ABOUT THE AUTHOR

James Warden was a teacher for forty years and retired in 2006. He now enjoys his retirement as much as he enjoyed his time in the education service and is catching up on those things which he left undone and ought to have done – in particular, his writing. He writes every morning between nine o'clock and noon, for thirty-six weeks of the year.

He is fortunate enough to be able to act in several Norwich theatres – the Maddermarket, the Sewell Barn and, with the Great Hall Players, at the Assembly House – and this experience informs his writing. His stage adaptation of Laurie Lee's *As I Walked Out One Midsummer Morning* was performed at the Sewell Barn Theatre in November 2009. His original play, *Letters from a Boy in the Trenches*, which was based on the letters of a WW1 soldier, was performed in Marchington, Staffordshire in 2015.

James is married – for the second time – and lives in Norfolk. He and his wife travel as much as possible. They have visited Italy (where they were married in 2002) several times, Canada, Bermuda, Egypt, India, the Czech Republic, New England, Poland, Slovenia, Antarctica, the Falkland Islands, Alaska, the Galapagos Islands, Australia and Switzerland. In 2018, they travelled across the USA on Route 66. They have also taken several holidays in various Mediterranean resorts – the basis for his first novel, *Three Women of a Certain Age*, which was published in July 2010.

During his years in education, he wrote about twenty play scripts for children. These included the one that formed the basis for his children's story, *The Great Gobbler and his Home Baking Factory at the North Pole*, which he wrote in 1982 and published in December 2010.

He has three sons by his first marriage, and they inspired three of his novels – *The Vampire's Homecoming*, published in 2011, *The One-eyed Dwarf*, published in 2012 and *The Haunting of Thornham Staithe*, published in 2022. With them and his first wife, he also travelled to the southern states of North America, France, Germany (West and East), Estonia and what was Czechoslovakia.

WRITING BY JAMES WARDEN

Stories of Our Time
Three Women of a Certain Age (2010)
The Age of Wisdom (2015)
Swinging in the Sixties (2016)

'Tales of Mystery and Imagination'
The Vampire's Homecoming (2011)
The First Rendlesham Incident (2017)
The Search for Edwin Drood (2020)
The Haunting of Thornham Staithe (2022)

Stories for Children
The Great Gobbler and his Home-Baking Factory at
the North Pole (2010)
The One-eyed Dwarf (2012)

Biography
The Boy in the Photograph: Bill Pieri's
autobiography (2014)
A Child of the Fifties: autobiography of my
childhood (2017)

Plays
As I Walked Out One Midsummer Morning
*(Adapted with the permission of Laurie Lee's estate
and performed at the Sewell Barn Theatre
in Norwich in November 2009.)*

Letters from a Boy in the Trenches
(Adapted from the letters home of Sydney Harrison
and performed by the Marchington
Amateur Dramatic Society in November 2015.)

The Bingham Detective Stories
Bingham's First Case (2018)
Bingham and the Runaway Wife (2019)
Bingham and the Odd Couple (2020)
Bingham and the Minister's Clerk (2021)
Bingham and the Traveller's Daughter (2022)
Bingham Along the Stuart Highway (2023)
Bingham Goes to Cannes
(To be published in 2024)
Bingham and the Lost Years
(To be published in 2025)
Bingham Crosses the Bar
(To be published in 2026)
Bingham's Dog Fight
(To be published in 2027)
Bingham's Cambridge Christmas
(To be published in 2028)

BINGHAM ALONG THE STUART HIGHWAY

BY

JAMES WARDEN

Grosvenor House
Publishing Limited

This book is published by
Grosvenor House Publishing Ltd
Link House
140 The Broadway, Tolworth, Surrey, KT6 7HT.
www.grosvenorhousepublishing.co.uk

A CIP record for this book
is available from the British Library

ISBN 978-1-80381-545-9

Chapter One
THE STUART HIGHWAY

It had been a long-cherished dream of the Binghams to visit Australia. With their holidays, it was Lina who usually did the planning; Bingham listened and encouraged his wife but rarely disagreed with her intentions. Only this time he had done so.

It was to be a tailor-made tour, latching on to what local operators had to offer but, largely, organising their own route and excursions. They'd flown into Melbourne, the 'garden city', where 'no one's more than a ten minute walk from a green spot' their guide had told them; they'd visited the Dandenong Mountains and had a ride on Puffing Billy, the 'world's oldest narrow gauge steam train'; they'd watched the 'parade of the Little Penguins' on Phillip Island, 'one of nature's most delightful rituals'; they'd made their way along the Great Ocean Road, stopping off at the local wineries whose soils produced 'some of the world's finest grapes' and, finally, descended into Adelaide, alongside the Murray River, the 'Mississippi of Australia', enjoying 'the panorama of vines, enchanting pastureland and some of the finest orchards in the world'. There was nothing modest about the view Australians held of their own country.

Bingham and Lina felt this from the beginning of their journey. It was still a young country, full of hope

1

and joy. Nothing paled, everything shone, and it was the easiest thing in the world to get along with the natives. Besides, it was one of only two places in the world – outside Britain – where Bingham found it possible to get a decent cup of tea.

In Adelaide, eschewing what amounted to a £36 a head breakfast at their hotel, on the advice of one of the staff, they ate breakfast at The Deli on Pulteney, which served two, golden-yolk eggs on fresh ciabatta plus coffee at £10 a head. It was a small café, frequented by people on the way to work, and the staff could not have been nicer. It was here that Lina tried, once again, to dissuade Bingham from his desire to drive to Alice Springs along the Stuart Highway.

"We can still catch a flight, Bing, and pick up our Uluru tour there – as planned," she urged in her best coaxing voice.

"It's the Stuart Highway, Lina – Australia's Route 66 – the mother road. We cannot but drive it."

"But the *Outback Tour* people take us south along the highway to Yulara, were we stay for a couple of days to view the sacred rock."

"Lina, we shall be on a coach – not driving ourselves. It won't be the same. Besides, Stuart went south to north," he added with a smile, "Imagine our excitement when we drive into Alice Springs in the footsteps of the great man. We'll have driven halfway across the great Red Centre."

And their journey had gone well. Even Lina, taking her turn at the wheel, enjoyed the drive. They'd savoured, however remotely from the cool of their air-conditioned four-wheel drive, what it might have been like to find oneself alone in this enormous desert of red sand with its canyons and cliffs, its colourful birds roosting noisily in the shattered branches of dead trees, listening to the din of thousands of insects and watching the intensity of the colours, which seemed to flare, pulse and fade as the day advanced.

"It's the emptiness that would frighten me if I was alone out here," said Lina, "There's something primeval about the place, and yet it is so beautiful: the light's so clear and the sky's so vast. Do you know – it's so wide that there are never enough clouds to cover it. Always there's a patch of blue somewhere."

Bingham was at the wheel when they came across the man. He was sitting, resting his back, against the corpse of a shattered tree that his car, an old Ford, had tried to climb. The vehicle was resting at a precarious angle. A gust of wind, thought Bingham, would send it clattering to earth. The driver looked rough (as well he might) but cheerful. He was dressed in a plaid shirt and a pair of faded dungarees that had been none too clean even before the accident. There was an open gash on his forehead from which blood had trickled and then dried on his cheek. More blood ran from his nose across a mouth and chin that were bruised.

"G'day," he called, trying to struggle to his feet as Bingham drew their vehicle to a halt. "I was hoping someone would breeze along. Bloody 'roo on the road. Swerved to avoid it – don't ask me why – and there I am halfway up the bloody tree."

"How did you get out of your car?" asked Lina, with a woman's eye to detail that always impressed Bingham.

"Had my seat belt on, fortunately, and found myself hanging there, upside down, my head cushioned against the roof. Once I'd snapped the belt loose, I was

OK – wriggled out through the window. The glass was shattered, yer see. Don't think I passed out – the wheels were still spinning when I climbed down. In fact, the radio was still playing."

As he spoke, the man crawled towards them on his hands and knees. Bingham and Lina reached down, placed their hands under his armpits and helped him to his feet. He stood, unsteadily.

"Nothing broken?" asked Lina.

"Don't think so – I can still wriggle my toes – but the car's a write-off."

"There're bits of broken glass in your face," said Lina, "Let me see if I can get them out."

Bingham looked at the wrecked Ford. What hadn't detached itself was either twisted or broken: the bonnet skewed at an awkward angle and the boot flapped up and down. It annoyed him that the radio was still playing; he reached into the car and switched off the music.

"Where were you going?" he asked.

"I was heading for Yulara – the Ayers Rock Resort. I've got a sheila there. You're on your way to Alice, are you?"

"We were," replied Lina.

"There's a roadhouse just off the highway. You can drop me there."

Bingham and Lina looked at each other because the same thought occurred to them both. Back home, you didn't just drop people off at a convenient roadside hostelry; on the other hand, back home you thought in dozens of miles, not hundreds.

"Let's get you into the station wagon", said Bingham, "and then I'll collect your gear. Oh, by the way, I'm George and this is my wife, Lina."

"Tony," said the man, "Tony McDonald – yeah, I know – no relation. Folks must have come out a long time ago."

Bingham wandered off to find Tony McDonald's possessions, which had been flung from the car: an old bag, four packs of beer and magazines, the type that contained some mild pornography and a few real-life stories. There was a tattered holdall, which Bingham supposed carried Tony McDonald's clothes and toiletries, two toolboxes and crates of wiring and other electrical items.

It was while he collected these things together that Bingham became aware he was hot – hot being a mild way of thinking about how he felt: sweat poured from under his hair, his shirt clung to him, especially around the neck, his watch bracelet itched the skin of his wrist and his feet rubbed against the rim of his desert boots. It was a prickly heat – dry and draining – and he'd been out of their vehicle for less than fifteen minutes. Bingham looked up. The sun was a red orb, diffused and spreading into the blue of the sky; the horizon was a haze. He flipped over the body of his travel watch; the thermometer was reading forty degrees.

Looking across at Tony MacDonald, now nestled safely in the back of their Holden, Bingham realised why they'd found him sitting in the shade of the broken car, however perilously it clung to the tree.

"Have some water, Bing," said Lina, when he'd finished stacking Tony MacDonald's belongings in the back of their wagon, "I take it, you're thinking what I'm thinking? Do you want me to do the driving for a while?"

"No, no. You're good at talking. Keep our guest entertained. I'm not stopping at the roadhouse. If we do, I have the feeling our friend will keep us drinking until it's dark. Yulara is a good one hundred and fifty miles from here and I want to get there before I fall asleep. This heat is overbearing."

Lina looked at her husband, wondering whether to question his decision and decided against it: Bingham's stubbornness was a byword in the family.

One and a half hours later, they drove into Yulara, by which time Lina had elicited from their guest that he was an electrician by training but "a jack-of-all-trades out here in the bush". He appeared to have no close family, such as a wife and children, but rotated his affections between a number of "sheilas", one of which was a young Aboriginal woman who worked as a cleaner at the Yulara resort. Given the apparent intimacy of his relationship with this young woman, Tony's views on "the Abos" – views he was only too eager to express – seemed strange.

"The trouble with Abos is they want bloody everything. They say the land's theirs by rights and when we give it back to them, they do nothing with it – except lease it back to us. They're some crafty buggers among 'em, too. Not that I've got anything personal against them. We get on well."

Tony went on in this vein for a while, and Bingham switched off, leaving Lina to present the liberal view, but it was a sore spot that was to emerge again and again, as Bingham discovered.

Yulara is simply a resort, a staging post for tourists visiting Uluru and Kata Tjuta. Along the route – the Lasseter Highway – their guest has startled the Binghams by pointing out Mount Connor, another huge rock that visitors mistake for the real thing they have travelled so many miles to see: Uluru, which they will photograph and salute with champagne as the sun sets and rises against its massive sides: Uluru, whose colours move from bright yellow through oranges and reds to a deep purple and, finally, brown when the sun sets.

Bingham had read about the rock and these pictures were running through his head as they pulled up outside Sails in the Desert, the hotel where it was planned they should stay on their tour from Alice Springs and where he and Lina hoped to find a bed that night.

It seemed that Tony MacDonald's "Abo girl" had accommodation in the staff quarters and the receptionist directed them through the resort. It was spotlessly clean and neatly landscaped. Looking at the canvas canopies that provided shade across the site, Bingham was reminded of the times Lina and he had spent aboard sailing ships. They made their way over brick-weaved squares between bleached-white trees, passing gift shops and beauty spas, cafes and restaurants. Every surface shone, whether it was the tiled floors, the metalled backs of chairs, the windows or the boulders that bordered the walkways.

Bingham was pleasantly surprised when they arrived in the staff accommodation, which he'd supposed to be primitive but was, in fact, newly, if not lavishly, furnished. Nellie Doolan, Tony's girl, was not in her room but the woman next door pointed them towards the theatre, "near where the lady who runs the art gallery lives" and where Nellie might be cleaning.

This was an apartment comprising several rooms, polished to the high shine of the rest of Yulara. It didn't look lived in, something Bingham deplored, and Nellie confirmed that it wasn't.

"At least, not at the moment. She's gone," she said, after giving Tony a cursory and polite, but not particularly passionate, hug.

"Gone where?" asked the jack-of-all-trades.

"No one knows. She vanished five days ago. Aren't you going to introduce me to your friends?"

Tony did and Bingham and Lina received a huge grin.

"How'd you do?" said the young woman, extending her hand that first Lina and then Bingham shook.

"Coming towards the end of the season, is it – closing early?" asked Lina.

"Our season hasn't started yet – not properly. Anyway, it's not like her to just go without a word," replied Nellie, supposing Lina was referring to the missing woman.

Bingham, perennially nosey, wandered from the short hallway into the living room of the apartment. It, too, shone: Bingham thought it glowed with polish – the wooden furniture, the tiled floors – and nothing was out of place.

"What was she like?" he asked, suddenly.

"I beg your pardon," answered Nellie Doolan from the hallway.

"What did she look like – the lady who lived here?"

Nellie came into the living room, followed by Lina and Tony, and stared at Bingham, a stare shared by his wife who was, also, taken aback at the bluntness of his question.

"You can see her?" asked Nellie Doolan.

In a certain way, he could. Bingham took in the shining surfaces and the angles at which such items as the various flower vases, the cigarette box, the stack of CDs, the stereo system and the fruit bowl on the dining table were placed. He couldn't imagine that the missing woman had a hair out of place. For the first time since entering the room he noticed, on one wall, a mirror without a smear, and beneath it a shelf holding a number of photographs.

"She was very smart – Mrs Helen."

It was the first time he'd heard her name.

"She was married?"

"Mr Lewis was killed a few years ago. It was an accident in the swimming pool."

"He drowned?"

"He slipped and must have knocked himself out. It was too late when they found him."

"Is Mrs Lewis still grieving?"

"I think not. Time heals. You can see her?"

"I thought she might be a very smart person – neat and trim."

"She was a short lady and very petite. She always dressed smartly and was very polite. She took care of herself."

"Did she always wear dresses?"

"Except when she was in the gallery hanging the work."

"She ran the art gallery?"

"She owned it."

"Aboriginal art?"

"Yes. It is popular with the tourists – like yourself."

There was a slight edge to her last two words occasioned, thought Bingham, by Nellie Doolan's view of tourists and, perhaps, their lack of appreciation of the art they bought.

"Perhaps we ought to go, Bing," said Lina, "Mr MacDonald needs to … clean up."

Bingham looked at the man they'd picked up and realised he was as they'd found him – dirty and dishevelled. He looked, too, at Nellie Doolan, who was standing beside him and for the first time, took her in. Nellie was short and stocky and no one could have called her beautiful – not if they judged beauty by outward appearance; but there was something about her large eyes and the way she stood that was appealing. Her black skin was spotless like the rest of the room and shone with a vigorous health, as did the mop of thick, curly hair.

Strange as it was, looking at Nellie and the room she cleaned, he could picture Helen Lewis clearly.

"It's all well," said Nellie, turning to Lina, "Your man has the Sight."

Bingham smiled. It was true that he could sense the occupant of a place they loved once he'd stood there for a while. He nodded at Nellie and pointed to a painting on the wall.

"Would you tell me about that?"

The painting consisted of a series of roughly concentric circles that seemed to be dropping from the sky; in the centre of each circle was a dark dot. Above them was a dark oblong from which tentacles spread outwards: some reached up, others down enclosing, or guiding, the circles. Scores of coloured dots linked the main features of the painting.

"It is Mother Earth and Father Sky," replied Nellie, "The three women are descending from the stars. Later, only two will return. It is at the equinoxes, when the sun crosses the celestial equator, that Father Sky and Mother Earth are joined as man and woman."

"What happened to the one who did not return?" asked Bingham.

"She was obliged to stay and play the role of Tya, the earth spirit."

"A prisoner in the world," said Lina, "Emu, the flightless bird."

A smile lit up Nellie Doolan's face as she realised that these two, these strangers, had taken the trouble to find out, to begin to understand, something of her heritage.

"Would you like to see the gallery? There are many paintings there."

"We'd love to," said Lina.

"Do you clean here every day?"

Lina looked at Bingham and frowned. She couldn't help herself: it was the second blunt question he'd asked.

"Why do you ask?"

"It's spotless, Nellie, and was when Mrs Lewis left five days ago and yet here you are, cleaning."

Nellie looked at Bingham, disappointment in her face, as though she'd seen an extraordinary quality in this man, only to find she was mistaken.

"I am worried," was all she said in reply, and turned away.

"She never suggested she was thinking of going anywhere?" Bingham persisted.

"No."

"But she would have done – at least with you?"

Bingham wasn't sure whether the frown deepened in respect or disgust, but Nellie Doolan said no more. She led them from the small apartment, along spruce walkways of terracotta slabs and between cream walls, to the art gallery, without another word, having dropped Tony MacDonald off on the way to clean himself.

In the gallery, surrounded by the work of her people, she seemed to loosen-up once again. The standard of display was precise and immaculate; appreciation of the artwork could be seen in every hanging; lizards scurried, rat kangaroos hopped, crocodiles devoured the moon, snakes slithered, fish glided and spiders waited to spring; and among these animals were the more homely paintings of women collecting bush tucker (berries, fruit and other foods such as honey) from the desert.

"These are the work of your people?" asked Lina.

"Yes. Mrs Lewis would buy from us."

Bingham wondered at the 'us'. He knew something, but very little, about the Aboriginal people; he knew there had been, at one time, hundreds of different tribes, each with their own language and, no doubt, warring with each other. Standing in Helen Lewis's living room, an idea had occurred to him, an idea he felt unable to pursue at that moment, such was his English reticence.

"I hope Mrs Lewis returns safely," he said, rather lamely he thought, when they left the gallery.

Nellie Doolan smiled a faint smile only and nodded as she locked the door.

"My husband and I are coming back to Yulara in a few days' time," said Lina, "We're only really here now because we came across Tony on the road."

"Yes. Thank you for bringing him. You are very kind."

The receptionist had been able to squeeze them in – a trick receptionists are often able to perform once they've kept you wondering while they scour the computer a few times to locate a "possible vacant room", thought Bingham – and the following morning Lina and Bingham set off on what was the final leg of their journey to Alice Springs, a distance of more or less 270 miles.

"A five-hour drive, sir. Take care – and see you in a few days," called the porter who'd been kind enough to park their Holden and bring it round to the front of the hotel when their time came to leave, adding with a grin, "Mind the wildlife."

The desert through which they drove was stark in the early morning light. From horizon to horizon the parched land stretched endlessly away. Bingham wondered how any living creature could possibly survive in such barrenness and afflicted by such an invasive heat. The temperature had exceeded 40 degrees the previous day and there was no doubt that, today, it would do likewise. Yet, the people and the beasts did survive out there: the hunters and the gatherers knew where to find their dinner. His mind was roving over the prospect of an isolated figure seeking refuge in this harsh land when Lina spoke.

The previous evening, neither he nor she had mentioned the disappearance of Helen Lewis, but Bingham knew his wife had something on her mind and wasn't surprised when she opened up.

"Why were you so blunt with Nellie Doolan, yesterday, Bing?"

"Blunt?"

"You know what I mean – 'What did Helen Lewis look like?', 'Why are you here?'"

"Is that what I said? I didn't mean to upset her. I liked Nellie."

"Don't evade my question. Why were you so blunt with her? Do you think there's something funny going on?"

"I don't think anything at all."

"You obviously do."

"What do you think, Lina?"

"Helen Lewis is not only an obviously intelligent woman she's also someone who's interested in what goes on around her – in her case, the Aboriginal culture."

"You think she's gone what's called 'walkabout'?"

"I don't think anything at all," replied Lina with a smile.

"Lina, I don't know what I think. It strikes me that what you suggest is the most likely, but why didn't she tell someone or leave a letter for Nellie?"

"I don't know."

"You and I wouldn't last five minutes out there."

"These locals have a familiarity with the red desert ... and it doesn't frighten them."

"Mm!" replied Bingham.

"I think Helen is a very spiritual person. The painting she obviously treasures – Mother Earth and Father Sky – is a mystical interpretation of Creation. The idea is timeless, now and forever, the connection of body and soul ... There comes a time in a woman's life when she has to decide her destiny. I don't mean the day-to-day; I mean the overall journey. For some it comes early: for others, later. For some, it comes naturally but for others it's brought about by a shock – something sudden that shakes you up and makes you think.

"For me, it came when I fell in love with you. I'll never forget the day we met – you standing in the foyer of the opera house looking vacant and me wondering who to talk to during the interval. I knew then what I'd been dreaming about since I was a young woman.

Things became clear to me, suddenly, but others have to search for the meaning they are seeking."

Bingham listened during Lina's reflection, not merely because he loved her but he sensed her concern for Helen Lewis. When she'd finished, he remained silent, watching the endless sands stretching away, dotted here and there by scrub and the tall, green trees that lined the road, their leaves looking as though they'd been spun from the black trunks.

"I'd come down to London see *The Turn of the Screw*," he said, eventually, "Britten's brilliant interpretation of James's novella. 'Another turn of the screw of human kindness'…"

"Pardon?"

"It's a phrase I picked up somewhere. I can't remember where. It must have been connected with the story … We'll stop for a coffee when we reach the Mt Ebenezer Roadhouse. We'll have covered about a hundred miles by then."

It was a habit of Bingham's to turn rapidly from one thought to another, and Lina smiled her tolerant smile, dashed with the knowledge that what she'd said had sunk in and was occupying his thoughts. Her husband pictured events and his mind, now, was watching two women – one standing in the foyer of the London Coliseum and the other in the Red Centre of Australia.

He didn't speak again until they reached the roadhouse, a large, wooden shack-type building with a corrugated roof painted white. Somehow, the intensity of the heat only seemed to be increased by the iron and the whiteness, but the interior was welcomingly cool.

Two things caught Bingham's eye simultaneously, and they were both notices. One advertised the *Imanpa*

Arts Gallery and the other, a double act, guided the visitor to either *Sheilas* or *Blokes*.

When he returned from the *Blokes,* Lina was already eyeing the *Things to Eat* board. Burgers and chips dominated the cuisine and his eye was caught by two items, in particular, the *Veggo's Delight* at $12.50 and something called a *Pig 'n Bumnut* at $9.50. Before his conversion to vegetarianism, Bingham would have tried the latter but he wasn't even tempted: meat had lost its appeal. The board also invited customers to *Grab Something From Hot Box*, but neither he nor Lina were ready to eat and so they settled for coffee: a small black for Bingham and a medium cappuccino for Lina.

The atmosphere of the place was functional and friendly. Despite the notice behind the bar advising customers that if they wanted 'to avoid injury, don't tell me how to do my job', which showed one person punching another, the staff couldn't have been more pleasant.

After they'd eaten, Lina wandered into the arts gallery and Bingham looked around. After viewing the bar, he strolled outside. The heat closed in on him at once and within minutes his clothes clung to his body; but this was experiencing the Australian desert. It was why Bingham had flown for 23 hours to be here, and he was pleased to be surrounded by a sense of place. A group of Aboriginals sat out under the shade of a tree of a kind unknown to Bingham, gossiping and drinking cola. Bingham smiled an acknowledgement but received no response.

The Imanpa Community owned the roadhouse. Bingham read this on a board nailed to one of the sun-baked walls. Was it here that Helen Lewis bought her works of art? Was she known here? Was Nellie Doolan known here?

He went back inside, meeting Lina on the way out. He knew at once she was perturbed about something. There was hesitation in her manner, as though she was torn between sharing the cause of her consternation or hiding it from him. Her better self won.

"I think you should see this, Bing."

Behind the bar was a notice bearing a photograph of Helen Lewis. The wording announced that she had been missing since March 20th, 2017, from the Ayers Rock Resort at Yulara. She was aged 48 and 5' 6" in height. She had a pale complexion, short brown hair and brown eyes. Helen was last seen wearing a white, cotton dress decorated with an abstract floral pattern and wearing sling-back shoes. Her friends and family need your help. Customers were asked Have you seen her? and urged to Contact Police 131 444. A large HELP completed the notice, which was by the look of it not an official one.

"Who asked you to put up the missing person notice," Bingham enquired of the barman.

"No idea, mate. We get them all through here – tourists, truckers, locals, anyone making a few quid travelling between Adelaide and Darwin, anyone within a radius of 300 miles, you might say. Rosie," he called across the room, "Do you know who wanted this notice put up?"

"Can't remember," replied a fat woman, clearing one of the tables.

"Was it a man or a woman?" asked Bingham.

"I said I can't remember. It may have been one of the other staff who took the notice."

"Does everyone live on site?"

"We come and go. We can ask around. Does it matter who put it up, mate?"

"I don't know," replied Bingham, "But it could matter a great deal."

Chapter Two

ALICE SPRINGS

Not one to be easily deterred, Bingham wandered first into the gallery, where he met the Frenchman who was selling and wrapping the Imanpu artwork displayed. It was a brief conversation, since a coachload of tourists were on-the-clock to buy and leave with their purchases: purchased, Bingham noticed later, at a fraction of the cost they would pay in Yulara.

"You know Helen Lewis, then?" he said, following his brief chat with the Frenchman that had established Bingham's credentials as a European.

"Oh yes," replied the Frenchman, "She buys from here. Nice lady: she always pays a fair price and has a genuine interest in the artists."

"Were you surprised she is missing?"

The Frenchman shrugged, as though the question was one only an Englishman would ask.

"She is a free spirit. She flies, she soars ... and she walks."

"You believe she's wandering in the desert."

"Wandering? With respect, you English will try to pin everything down and you are mistaken. Wandering? You speak as if Helen is lost. She is not: she is Dreaming. You'll have to excuse me, I ..."

"Yes, of course," replied Bingham, aware of the coachload lined up behind him, as he cut off with his painting of *4 People gathering honey ants* by Nellie Mick.

Collecting Lina and the 'missing' poster on the way, He approached the group of Aboriginals he'd seen earlier.

"Excuse me," he said, placing Nellie's painting on the bench in front of them, "Is this work by one of you?"

Scarcely looking at the painting, the group of artists shook their heads. They seemed uneasy, as though Bingham had encroached upon their privacy, which he was the first to acknowledge he had.

"I'm sorry. I don't wish to intrude ... We met Nellie Doolan at Yulara. She seemed concerned that her friend, Helen Lewis, has disappeared. Did she come here?"

It was a question, blunt enough, to which he knew the answer. He showed the poster around, watching their faces. They were expressionless: mouths frozen, eyes glazed. Eventually, one of the older women spoke.

"She comes here. She buys our work."

"When did you last see her?"

The woman muttered something Bingham heard as 'birak'. He didn't like to push his enquiries, but Lina did.

"'Birak'", she said, "We don't understand."

The group of people smiled within their circle. The older woman spoke for them.

"Summer," she said, laughing, "She comes in summer."

"For many paintings and your crafts?" Lina pursued.

"In birak and burnur," replied the woman, and the group around the picnic bench laughed again.

"Summer and autumn," said Lina, with a smile, "She buys in the summer for the paintings she sells in the winter?"

"And you last saw her in the summer – birak," said Bingham, "Thank you. Thank you very much."

As Lina and Bingham returned to the bar to hand back the poster, he smiled and said:

"I didn't know you spoke Aboriginal."

She nudged him with her elbow and laughed.

"There's a lot you don't know about me."

Back in their Holden and on the way to Alice Springs – the sun-soaked road stretching endlessly, yet beautifully, before them and the trees Bingham had admired on their way from Yulara, and which he'd now been told by the barman were called desert bloodwoods, moving slightly in a fresh-sprung breeze – Lina asked:

"Do you really think she's missing, Bing?"

"Someone does – or thinks she might be. Otherwise, why put up the poster? There's another stop on the way, the Stuart's Well Roadhouse, where I thought we might have lunch. We'll see if someone's dropped off a poster there."

They had, but the Binghams' enquiries produced less than they'd discovered at the Mt Ebenezer. The proprietor had a reputation for liking animals: camels, kangaroos, emus. Whenever one was found injured on the highway – and this happened often – he rescued the animal; if a baby was discovered motherless, he brought it in to Stuart's Well, deep in the Northern Territory. The establishment was a sanctuary and a business.

But no one at Stuart's Well could remember seeing Helen Lewis: it wasn't one of her stop-offs.

Alice beckoned.

Bingham had dreamed of this town ever since reading Neville Shute's book, *A Town Like Alice*. It was part of the unconscious clutter he had brought with him from his youth. It was one of those places he knew he'd visit one day, without ever wondering how or when. He had no expectations. People with expectations were likely to be doomed to disappointment; life had taught him to be cautious. He wanted only to be here, soaking in the atmosphere of the town and coming to a sense of place.

The foothills of the MacDonnell Range enclosed the town, which was bathed in the flaxen glow of early evening. It was still very hot, but the slight breeze cooled the air sufficiently to make walking the streets pleasant. On Anzac Hill, two flags fluttered. Bingham could see the flags without discerning which ones they were, but they'd find out tomorrow when he and Lina intended to book a tour: the Hill, the Overland Telegraph Office, the Flying Doctor Service.

He arrived full of anticipation and just a tad annoyed. One of the men working at the Stuart's Well Roadhouse had warned them not to go out alone in Alice after dark. It was the only place in the civilized world where such advice had been urged upon them. In other places, they'd received the same cautions and in some had been accompanied by security guards on guided tours; but ignoring the warnings and venturing out together, dressing more or less like the locals and not waving cameras around, Lina and he had always found people welcoming and had felt quite safe.

Matt Toohey, the man who'd warned them, was reluctant to be specific; but Bingham, equally reluctant not to walk out at night, was determined to find out why the town was supposed to be dangerous. Unable to locate a carpark, he drove their vehicle into a side street he thought might be out of the way and they walked to Todd Mall, where Lina's phone told them there would be tourist information.

The mall was air-conditioned, cool as a summer's day at home, and *Sybil's Supa Snacks* provided them with a cold drink. It also provided them with their first piece of gossip when Bingham asked a woman at the next table where they might find the police station.

"You go down Parsons and you'll find the police on the corner of Bath and Parsons – it's not far. Why, you lost something?"

"No, no," replied Bingham, "We were warned about going out alone at night and wondered why."

"You're poms, aren't you? You don't want to worry about it. They only go for the wealthy tourists – the Japs," the woman answered with loud laugh.

"They?"

"The Abos. They're after money for drink – as though the government don't give them enough in handouts."

"My wife's joking," cut in the woman's husband, obviously hot under the collar, "Tourists always ask the same question – 'is it safe to go out alone at night in Alice?' Of course, it is – as safe as anywhere else in the world. It worries me that the Northern Territory is getting this kind of reputation. We're no worse than anywhere else."

"Thank you," said Lina, who was eager to avoid a clash between husband and wife.

"Oh, come on, Sid, you know very well there're drunks in the streets and down on the Todd riverbed ..."

"Keep your voice down, Mabel. That problem was addressed years ago, and the police keep a high profile there, now."

"Exactly what I'm saying. Perhaps you'd tell me why they need to keep a high profile?"

"Thank you for your advice," Lina urged, rising from her seat, "We'll bear it in mind."

"You do that. If you plan to go out at night, go out with friends or drive," bawled Mabel.

Outside, on Parsons Street, Lina took Bingham's arm and leaned against his shoulder, laughing.

"You'd never get a job as a marriage guidance counsellor, Bing."

"I'd never want one, Lina, but I think the angst was well imbedded in that couple before I asked my question. Let's have a look round. I quite fancy seeing this Todd River."

The term 'river' was a misnomer: the Todd was as dry as the proverbial bone, the white, sandy bed cracked and broken by drought. Along the bed, a few sedges struggled to survive and further up the bank grew the bushes known as mallees, their shiny leaves a protection against the relentless sun. Bingham wondered, for the umpteenth time since they'd arrived, how anyone could survive beyond the town.

The bustle of voices in the Mall was behind them and from beyond the far bank of the river came faint sounds of a different kind of life. Bingham's encroaching deafness kept them from him, but Lina heard vague rustlings, the scuttling of insects on the bushes and, perhaps, from further out the howl of a dingo or the chomping of a wallaby feeding.

Groups of Aboriginals lounged on the dry banks, taking in the cool sun of the early evening or simply waiting. A few were gathering sticks. Watching them, Bingham saw boredom, boredom stemming from loss: after the settlers arrived and claimed the land to raise their sheep, a way of life was lost forever.

"There's a precinct not far from here that I'd like to take a look at," said Bingham. "I glimpsed it just before we parked."

"We'll need to check in, soon," said Lina, "Double Tree by Hilton is expecting us late afternoon. It's on the other side of the river, just past the Botanic Gardens, near the golf course."

"Another world, then," he replied, with a wry smile.

And it was: 'high-end indigenous art', 'spacious guest rooms', 'two tennis courts', 'plush bedding', a '24-hour fitness centre', 'a heated outdoor pool and spa', 'Indian-Thai fusion dining', an '18-hole golf course' and 'within walking distance of downtown Alice Springs'.

"Yes, sir," said the man at the reception desk in answer to Bingham's question, "but we don't advise our guests to walk around there at night."

In their room, with its 'mountain and garden views', Lina and Bingham unpacked. However short their stay in any one place, they were both obsessive about hanging their clothes.

Afterwards, while Lina contacted their children on the 'high-speed internet access', Bingham sat quietly by the window pretending he was taking in the view but actually thinking about Helen Lewis. It was silly to be troubled.

He knew he was an old fool, softened by a western lifestyle. Just because he couldn't imagine himself venturing into the desert didn't mean that others lacked both the nerve and the desire. Wasn't it very likely that a woman who obviously respected the Aboriginal culture might want the experience? She was at that certain age and widowed only a few years previously: restless, no doubt, and eager to make something of what was a new life.

"Do you mind if I have a wander?" he asked, after a while.

Lina didn't, since she was absorbed in chatting with their youngest son, Ben, a chemist who worked in Norwich at the John Innes Centre.

"I'll meet you in the restaurant, Bing. We're booked for 6.30."

They ate in the Hanuman restaurant and Bingham was pleased to see that the vegetarian dishes were reasonably priced. It always annoyed him at home when he and Lina were forking out nearly as much as meat eaters, given the cost of that ingredient. He enjoyed a dhingri mutter at $18.50 and Lina tucked into a tadka dahl at $11.50.

He knew she was troubled by what he intended to do that evening and waited. Eventually, she expressed her concern.

"I've been chatting with Ben," she said, "and a friend of his had a spot of bother when he was here a year ago. He said it's not the kind of place where you'd expect to be mugged but there was a lot of drunkenness. His friend turned a corner and found thirty teenagers, all drunk and spoiling for a fight."

"What happened?"

"He ran."

"I met a young man in the bar ..."

"You went for drink before dinner?"

"Yes."

"Without me?"

Bingham was never sure whether his wife was genuinely outraged or merely posturing when she reacted adversely to the idea that he might have left her alone and wandered into a bar. Not one to pursue an issue, he continued:

"I found myself chatting to one of the waiters. He kept his voice low but was quite open with me. He called me 'dude" ..."

Lina laughed: anyone less a 'dude' than her husband, she found it hard to imagine.

"He said he'd been born and bred here and didn't recommend anyone to go out after dark: lots of drunks, lots of fights, cops nowhere to be seen and burnouts."

"Shall we leave the car here and take a taxi?"

It was Bingham's turn to laugh. He admired his wife: she had pluck. He'd always thought that it was one of the reasons he'd married her.

The taxi driver was as chatty as any of the other natives Lina and Bingham had come across: instantly friendly seemed to sum up the attitude of the country.

"You guys in a coach party?"

"No, we drove here from Adelaide," replied Bingham.

"Left your car at Double Trees, did you? Don't blame you. You can't be too careful at night in Alice."

"So, we've been told," said Bingham.

"It's like anywhere else, you know. It's just a matter of using your common sense – like you've left your car behind. Sensible. Recently, we had some (shall we say, international?) travellers who left their car, full of their belongings, in a small carpark in the north of Alice. This carpark's OK during the day but it's totally vacant at night. The car was there for eight days! When they returned to get it, they found it broken into. They lost all their belongings! Now, if they'd left their car in a sensible location, they wouldn't have had half the issues they met, would they?"

"No, I suppose not," replied Bingham in as mild a voice as he could muster, since he subscribed to the old-fashioned notion that you ought to be able to leave your car anywhere you fancied without it coming to harm.

There was no time for further warnings because the journey took slightly more than five minutes. Pulling alongside the curb of the main street, the taxi driver turned to the Binghams

"Here's my card. If you folks need a lift back, I can be here in no time. Enjoy your evening. That'll be $20."

Lina, realising Bingham was unlikely to be leaving a tip for a five-minute ride that had cost the equivalent of £13, touched her husband gently on the arm and reached for her purse.

"Daylight robbery at night," said Bingham as the taxi pulled away.

"Petrol is expensive here, Bing."

"Yes. Are you OK? Nervous?

"A bit, but you can't let it worry you, can you? It's either a free world or it's not. The bully boys can't have it their own way or all our fathers fought for is thrown to the winds."

Despite the warnings and notwithstanding his unease, Bingham was looking forward to their stroll. A stroll with Lina was always a joy and he knew Alice

Springs was a true icon of Australia. This was one reason he'd wanted to drive along the Stuart Highway, which links Darwin in the north with Adelaide in the south. The road had brought them to the town that had such strong associations with the European pioneers who opened up the country. It had come into being in 1870 as a key station on the Overland Telegraph Line.

He knew, too, that the town was packed with Aboriginal culture: not least of which were the idiosyncratic dot designs, complex maps showing the routes of the Dreamtime beings. One of Australia's most famous Aboriginal artists, Albert Namatjira, had lived here.

These thoughts in mind, Bingham led his wife from the main street into an open precinct of shops, bars and cafes. In tourist areas such places are usually open at night and Bingham was a man who lived in hope. These were not entirely shattered, but slightly marred, when they found many of the places they'd glimpsed when they arrived closed.

But there was, at least, one gallery open – or almost open. A fat, red-headed woman was on the point of locking up when Lina spoke to her.

"We seem to be too late. Are you open tomorrow?"

The woman paused only slightly before answering, as though her mind was elsewhere or she was tired after a long day.

"You want to look around?"

"No, no, not if you've finished for the day. We hoped there might be more places open."

"There will be when the season gets in full swing. It's not worth folks while 'til the weather cools a bit … Come in. I've nowhere to go. I'm Marje, by the way."

29

Lina introduced them and they entered the shop, which was alive with Aboriginal arts: paintings, sculptures, fabrics. While Lina looked round and chatted, Bingham watched the woman. She was fat, but not in a sloppy way: big and firm would be a fitting description, thought Bingham, and 'in good condition'. He wasn't sure where that phrase sprung from, at first, and then realised it was from a play, *Alfie*, which he'd had a minor role in some years before at the Sewell Barn Theatre in Norwich. Recalling himself to the moment, he said:

"Do you buy your work from the locals?"

"The Arrernte – yeah, too right. They make a good living out of it and so do I. You folks from England, are you?"

"Yes."

"G' luck. You'll enjoy our country. Me – I was born and bred here. Not in Alice. I come from Adelaide, myself, but I've lived here for years."

"So, you get on with the locals?"

"You mean the Abos? Sure. You get the odd problem with tourists, but if some of these girls walk around with their tits hanging out what do they expect? It's an invitation, isn't it? On display and up for grabs, you might say."

Bingham was quiet and hoped Lina would follow suit: silence encouraged the voluble and he liked listening to people.

"I've no urge to live anywhere else. Got everything I need here. Travelled as far as Sydney once – ten years ago – but I don't like big cities – smaller the place, nicer the people. There's plenty to do here, when you've got the time to do it – drive around, go fishing, camp-overs.

Can I offer you folks a drink? Always got a drink on hand in the gallery – softens folks up – but don't feel obliged to buy anything. It's nice talking to you. The wine's up from Adelaide – Murdoch Hill Chardonnay – $25 a bottle – it's a nice drop of plonk. A friend of mine – a trucker – drops it off when he's here."

Lina brought over a table runner that she'd been stroking for some time.

"We'll take this. It's lovely."

"The Abo artists are clever buggers. They turn their hands to anything," said Marje, and added with a laugh, "Don't suppose they've got much use for runners out in the bush. Do you fancy a boomerang?"

"Sorry," said Bingham, aware Marje had spoken to him but hadn't really heard what she'd said.

"A boomerang," repeated Marje, laughing even louder, "or a didgeridoo?"

"No, I'll leave it for the moment. Thank you."

Marje eventually, but in an unhurried way, led them from the shop and directed them to a local bar where she was sure they'd find "a decent drink" and "enjoy the evening". Bingham was left brooding and faced with Lina's inevitable question when he'd been quiet for some time:

"What are you thinking?"

"Nothing really."

"You must have been thinking something."

"I was just thinking how different those two women are. They do the same work, they're both owners of galleries that specialise in Aboriginal art but as personalities they're chalk and cheese."

"You were wondering how they deal with their artists?"

"You can read me like a book, can't you?"

"I hope so – we've been married over thirty years," replied Lina, putting her arms round Bingham and kissing him lightly on the lips.

The rest of the evening was uneventful. As always, they enjoyed each other's company in a foreign place. The walls of the bar were decorated by pictures of the early pioneers: those men – and one woman – who had founded the town. The table mats bore the same faces.

On their way back, they found a policeman at the door of a cheap liquor store. Bingham didn't stop to ask the question he whispered to Lina.

They walked back to their hotel, lingering on the Tuncks Road Bridge to gaze along the riverbed. A group of Aboriginal men were sprawled on the grass, each grasping a bottle; another leaned back against the trunk of a ghost gum tree. Occasionally, they heard the screams of women arguing. Further along the riverbed, groups squatted. It seemed to be the favourite gathering place of the dispossessed. Bingham had read that the Todd flooded every ten years and wondered how long it would be before the next one.

Chapter Three
THE GALLERY

Their first day in the town was to have been their free day, but the time spent at Yulara had dispensed with that plan and so Lina and Bingham woke to their guided tour of Alice Springs.

The coach driver who was also their guide was a knowledgeable young man. A Scot, he'd come to Alice on holiday, fell in love with a local girl and stayed on. A degree in Aboriginal culture later, he felt qualified to talk about his new country and its hopes for the future.

By mid-morning the heat was touching 43 degrees and the flies had descended in their millions – or so it seemed to Bingham. Lina and he were both protected by the veils they'd brought with them on the advice of Lina's sister who had family in Australia. It was impossible to be outside and unprotected: the flies were relentless, landing as they did on every inch of exposed skin to suck the salt from the sweat of the tourists.

From Anzac Hill, where Bingham now saw that the two flags were the Australian national one and the cultural flag of the Aboriginal people, Alice Springs looked to be no more than a scattering of houses in a bleak, arid land by a dried-up riverbed. Bleached trees and bushes were scattered but grew everywhere: the ghost gums, the desert bloodwoods and the mallees. As tough, Bingham thought, as the people who lived there.

"On Anzac Day, the road up the hill is lined with people and the whole hillside is crowded: women and children as well as the blokes. You can't find a space to stand. It's a big thing for us. Lots of folks lost in the wars," answered the guide, Rob, in answer to Bingham's question.

Bingham had commented on the signs that lined the road: each sign commemorating a conflict somewhere in the world, a conflict in which Australians had fought alongside soldiers from other parts of the Commonwealth. The ties that bind us, thought Bingham, were stronger than those that divided nations.

"You asked about the Aboriginals. We know things started badly, but it's no good looking back. The first people to land here were the scum of the earth. Two hundred years ago, they thought that criminals couldn't be rehabilitated and so Britain dumped them here. You can imagine the bloodshed there was in the grab for land. They thought the indigenous inhabitants weren't even human – you know, didn't have a soul – and they openly hunted them down like animals. Of course, the Aboriginals had the upper hand at first – they knew the territory and could escape easily into the bush – but once the Native Police got on the job they had no chance."

"Native Police?"

"The settlers paid Aboriginals from other clans to hunt their own people down. They knew their ways, of course, and could track them through the bush. It was massacre after massacre …Yeah, OK, we'll be off in a while."

Rob turned to speak to the groups of tourists eager to be on their way, and Bingham wandered off the coach to find Lina. He came across her reassuring a young woman who was fussing about the flies and her veil.

"I don't think it's meant to be attractive," she was saying, "let it hang as low as possible. That way, you'll keep them off your chest."

Bingham looked at the young woman who was wearing a sleeveless blouse cut low to show her breasts. Flies were settling everywhere. He smiled, relieved that he didn't feel the need to look appealing.

Back on the coach, everyone relaxed in the air-conditioned interior and sipped water, an activity Bingham found to be relentless; their guide kept bottles of the stuff in a cooler in the coach's storage space. Enough, Bingham thought, to stock an average supermarket at home.

Dust whirling from under the wheels, they set off for the Overland Telegraph Station where Bingham hoped to find the cup of Northern Territory Roasted Coffee promised by Rob. He did and sat drinking it, accompanied by a vanilla slice, with their guide, while Lina wandered from the station master's residence to his kitchen and on to the barracks, the buggy shed, the battery room and shoeing yard.

She knew Bingham would remain disturbed about the 'not going out alone at night in Alice Springs' dictum. It went against the grain with a man who valued the freedom for which their fathers had fought, and Bingham had been in conversation with Rob since they boarded the coach.

"It's the drink," Rob was saying over his coffee with the persistently inquisitive Bingham, "It's not a question of not being able to hold their drink; it's more that, biologically, their bodies are not adapted to processing the stuff. It'll take a generation or two more, I guess.

"But there's no question of Alice not being safe. I live here, dammit. OK – if I hear screaming from down on the riverbed, do I go to investigate? Of course, not! Would you go up a dark alley at night at home if you heard someone screaming? Probably not: you don't know what you might come across. Are you going to take a look around, George? We've got about half-an-hour left before we set off for the Flying Doctor Service."

"Yes, I suppose I am," replied Bingham.

"After all, you are on holiday. Go and find your wife."

Bingham found Lina in the post telegraph office where during the time the station was the essential link between north and south Australia operators received and repeated confidential messages of births, deaths and world news, quietly reading the Morse code with their ears and speaking it onward with their fingers.

"A lonely life, Lina," said Bingham, taking a shot of his wife standing by the operator's desk wearing her anti-fly veil.

"When it was fully operational there was a cook, a blacksmith cum stockman, four telegraph operators, the station master and his family and a governess for the children," replied Lina, "I keep wondering what it was like being the governess."

"Lonely, I imagine, unless she got on with the station master's wife. I've never minded loneliness myself and nor did my mother after my father died so suddenly. She always said, 'alone but never lonely', whenever I asked."

"She was a woman who had so much going on in her head."

"Yes," replied Bingham, "she was."

Talking about his mother, he suddenly felt easier about Helen Lewis. She was someone with 'so much going on in her head'. It wasn't, perhaps, surprising that she had decided to go walkabout before the tourist season opened in earnest.

His feeling of ease swelled during their return to Alice, where they'd planned to eat in the town rather than the hotel. A bar had attracted their attention the previous evening – a bar that promised to brim with locals during the day, and the Binghams enjoyed eating where the locals ate wherever they went: it was always cheaper.

Rob dropped them off and wished them luck. Approaching the bar, two things caught their eye: a small crowd bustling on the other side of the street and a notice that had appeared overnight. The notice offered 'kangaroo burgers and wedges @ $19.95' and 'Skippy, Dundee, croc and roo skewers @ $16.95'. Living in Alice wasn't cheap, thought Bingham, and this bar might not offer a great deal for vegetarians.

Nevertheless, in they went to a warm welcome from the barman who ushered them to a table by the window, where a young waitress dropped off a menu and took orders for their drinks. It was while Lina was wondering whether to have 'roo steak, egg and chips' without the roo steak but with an extra egg, that the policeman walked into the bar.

He was immaculate in his starched and ironed uniform, a vision of blue and white: a lean young man whose smartness contrasted sharply with the casual dress adopted by most of the customers. Here was a copper who demanded your attention, thought Lina, who gave the officer a smile as he passed by on his way to the bar.

The gaze of the crowd across the street had followed him. Looking out of the window, Bingham noticed this fact, as Lina watched the reaction of the barman who seemed alarmed. Even the waitress paused and turned to look on her way to another table. Bingham could hear nothing, and lip read less but sensed the urgency in the policeman's voice. His enquiries completed, the officer turned, surveyed the bar and left.

"What was that about?"

"The lady we met yesterday hasn't turned up to open her gallery. The police officer wondered if the barman knew anything," replied Lina.

"Did he?"

"He said it was unlike her, but perhaps she was unwell."

"Why the concern?"

"The young woman who works there couldn't get into the gallery and her boss, Marje, always phoned if she wasn't coming to work for any reason."

'Marje' and 'Rob', thought Bingham, wondering whether Australians ever gave their surnames.

"It shouldn't be too difficult to find out whether she's ill in bed," he said.

"The policeman had checked. She isn't at home."

By the time the Binghams finished their lunch the small crowd had dispersed, their curiosity waning in the heat of the afternoon. Lina and her husband stood on the pavement outside the gallery, scorched by the glare of the sun that had turned the blue of the sky into a white sheet of metallic heat.

"What a shame," he said, "I was wondering whether to buy one of her didgeridoos for Ben."

"And how were we to get it home?"

"Check it in as any musician would do."

"I suppose so. Shall we get on with our own walkabout?"

The heritage trail they'd planned to follow beckoned: the Flynn Memorial Church, Adelaide House, the Residency, Old Stuart Town Gaol, Old Hartley Street School and the National Pioneer Women's Hall of Fame were on their schedule for that afternoon, and it was several hours later before they stopped off at their lunchtime bar for a beer prior to returning to Double Trees to wash away the sweat and change their clothes for the evening meal.

Glancing across at Marje's gallery, Lina noticed it was open and suggested that they went over immediately. There was no one in the shop, but the bell rang as they entered, and Bingham had only just picked up one of the smaller didgeridoos and was turning it over in his hands when the woman spoke.

"You folks looking for a genuine instrument, you've found one."

The voice boomed, and there was nothing feminine about the speaker who must have appeared from what Bingham supposed was an office at the back of the gallery. She wore a pair of jogging trousers and a sweatshirt. Her hair was cut short, her eyebrows were massive, and so she had a manly appearance. She filled the gallery.

Watching her husband stare, Lina responded quickly:

"We're pleased to see you open. We understood that Marje has ... disappeared."

"You didn't find the gallery open this morning, did you? It caused a bit of a stir, I understand. Even got the local bobby on the move. Sorry about that. I didn't get Marje's note until I got back. I'd been out at the place feeding the joeys. Then my chicks escaped, and I had a job rounding them up. Couldn't leave them loose – not with so many dingoes about. Even so, I couldn't catch all the little buggers. Oh, my name's Em, by the way. Pleased to meet you. You're from back home, I take it."

"Where is Marje," asked Bingham.

Em gave him a strange look, as though she would have preferred Bingham to ask about the animals.

"She's gone walkabout, I expect."

"Is that what the note said?"

Another strange look followed, and Lina intervened, giving Bingham a quick glance.

"My husband is only concerned because we came across another closed gallery in Yulara and then saw the lady was reported missing."

"You don't need to worry about Marje. She's at home in the outback."

"You look after strays, do you?" enquired Bingham, eager to mend the bad impression he'd given.

"We must be the only country in the world that kills off its national emblem. You're always finding kangaroos on the side of the road. These bloody truckers need to be more careful. There's no need for it. Some of those they leave dead are mothers. My joeys came from the pouch of two of them I found just outside Alice."

"They must keep you very busy," suggested Lina.

"Too true. I'll have to get the girl to run this place. Marje knows that. I can't do everything."

"Is she likely to be away long?" asked Bingham.

"Who knows? She doesn't get really busy until May when the weather gets a bit cooler. They're our busiest months – May through to August. Then, once we get into spring and summer it's too bloody hot."

"Have you and Marje lived here long?"

"I was born here on a station just outside Alice. My father's place. He's dead now. It's where I keep my orphans. Marje came up from Adelaide. She's been here a few years now. Gets on well with the indigenous people. They see eye to eye, if you know what I mean."

Bingham didn't but took it that Marje was very direct and supposed the artists she dealt with appreciated the fact.

"Did she go out alone?"

"You mean did she take one of the Abos as a guide? I doubt it, but one of her suppliers may have obliged. I said – don't worry about her. We know our country."

"So, you're not going to report her missing?"

"Marje'd go crazy if I did anything like that – believe me! Are you wanting that didgeridoo? I need a smoke and I don't like doing it in here with all this stuff about. Marje'd go nuts."

"Our son – one of our sons – plays the saxophone and Bing thought he might like one of these. May we take a look before we choose?"

"Sure. I'll be on the street. How many kids have you got?"

"Four – the two boys, Ben and Paolo, and the girls, Cecilia and Fiorenza – they're twins. The girls work in London. Fiorenza is a researcher for the BBC and Cecilia is a politician's secretary. Ben's a chemist and lives in Norwich and …"

"Paolo – sounds like a bloody rabbit. I don't have any of them at the moment, but they come and go."

It was apparent from the glazed look in her eyes that Em had lost interest in Lina's account of her children soon after the mention of Paolo. Her sudden interruption confirmed her indifference.

"You don't have a family?" asked Lina, slightly nettled, thought Bingham.

"Not unless you count the livestock. I suppose you might look on the sheep, a couple of cows, a nanny goat, a cat or two, a few possums, the two roos and the joeys as family. I'll have my smoke. Now, if you don't mind."

Em left the gallery abruptly and Bingham watched her roll a fat cigarette with one hand. A non-smoker himself, it was a skill he'd always admired. She waited outside while he and Lina selected what she considered to be the nicest and the most practical of the Aboriginal instruments: "nicest" being the most decorative and "most practical" being the one most easily transported through customs and on flight. Nothing, thought Bingham, if not sensible.

"Good choice," said Em, returning to the gallery. "Mind you, they're all bloody good. These people know their business. Have you ever played one?"

"No, but we've a visit planned to Kuranda later on our trip and I think we'll get the chance there."

"That's Tjapukai territory. They're bonza folk. You'll love them. You wouldn't like to come out and see my place one day, would you? I could introduce you to the family."

"We'd love to," said Lina, quickly, "We've a trip to Uluru planned and that will take a day or two but we're not on the clock. Perhaps, when we return, we could get in touch."

"That'll be good. You'll like my family. Here, if you leave your purchase with me, I'll see that the girl gets it bubble-wrapped and boxed. It'll be safer when those bastards at the airport start throwing your luggage around. You can pick it up some other time."

Walking back to their hotel, Double Trees, Bingham said:

"Marje and Em – don't they use surnames in Australia?"

"Do we, *back home*, when we introduce ourselves to strangers?"

"I suppose not. It's funny, isn't it, how they use the term, *back home*, especially people like Em, who's never lived there?"

Later that evening – washed, changed and fed – Lina and Bingham, more confident than previously, wandered back into Alice. It was the pleasure of the stroll that drew them rather than any expectation they might pick up their didgeridoo but, as it happened, the gallery lights were still on.

Em's stout bulk was immediately recognizable. She was talking to a bony-faced, red-haired, young man who seemed agitated, judging by the way he was fiddling with the cuffs of his jacket. Every now and then, he would lurch back on one heel and then thrust himself forward as though he was about to punch the woman; then, his head would drop for a moment before he lifted it to push his glasses back to the bridge of his nose.

"They seem to be having a row, Bing."

"What are rows, Lina," replied Bingham, acknowledging, with a smile, the fact that he and she had never had one.

"Perhaps we should come back later?"

"Perhaps we should go in now."

When the doorbell rang, both Em and the young man turned: anger on his face, relief on hers. Bingham remained silent, deliberately, but Lina, keen to calm the situation, smiled and spoke.

"We're just out for a stroll. We saw the lights and wondered if the didgeridoo was ready to collect."

"Sure," replied Em, and quickly disappeared into the office.

"I'm George Bingham and this is my wife, Lina," said Bingham, quickly, extending his hand as he spoke.

"What's that to me?" replied the young man who turned quickly and made for the door.

Bingham reached to open it for him, effectively barring his way.

"Excuse me," he expostulated, pushing Bingham aside.

"Are you Marje's son?"

"What's that to you?"

"You seem upset. I take it your concerned with your mother's disappearance."

"I don't know who you are or by what right you say my mother has *disappeared*."

His stress on the last word seemed to be a denial – at least to Bingham, who pursued the issue, his arm clutching the door handle.

"It might be worth sharing your concern."

"With you? I don't know who the hell you are or why you stick your nose into my affairs but in all decency, if you really are concerned, I suggest you let me pass."

His agitation was very apparent now: he fiddled with the sleeves of his jacket, lowered his head, once again, like a charging bull and then lifted it high to push his glasses upwards.

"Have you spoken to the police?"

"I'm not compelled to answer your questions. I'm not even obliged to speak to you. Who are you?"

At that moment, Em returned with the Binghams' parcel.

"What's going on?"

"I was enquiring about the young man's … Sorry, I didn't catch your name," said Bingham.

"You didn't catch it because I didn't give it to you."

"Henry, there's no need to take that tone. I'm sure Mr Bingham meant well."

"I really don't care what he meant. It's none of his business."

"You are concerned about your mother, then?"

"You are persistent – bloody persistent."

"So, my wife tells me. Look, I don't want to upset you any further and I apologize if I've done so, but if I can be of any help at all please get in touch. Lina and I are staying at the Double Trees for the next day or so."

"You're tourists, aren't you? Just go and gawp at your bloody rock and piss off."

With this final exhortation that Bingham should leave him alone, the young man barged past and disappeared into the night.

"Sorry about that," said Em, "He's a bit headstrong."

"Perhaps we shouldn't have interfered," said Lina, soothingly.

"Perhaps not," said Bingham, looking closely at the parcel Lina had taken from Em and noting the name on the invoice note she had stuck on the outside ready for the customs people. He noted 'Marjory Fink' as the proprietress of 'Aboriginal Arts: Alice Springs'. "Thanks, Em," he continued, "By the way, I didn't catch your last name."

"That's because I didn't give it to you. Everyone around here is on first name terms. It's Hawker – Emily Hawker – although the last person to call me Emily was my mother, and she's long gone, poor soul. I'll see you around, then, and take you out to see the family."

"We're looking forward to it," said Lina, "I love possums."

Sitting in what considered itself an upmarket bar on the way back to their hotel, each of them drinking a schooner of beer that had cost the equivalent of £8 a pint, Bingham looked at Lina and Lina looked at Bingham. She burst out laughing.

"You were persistent, Bing."

"I acknowledge the fact."

"And we are on holiday."

"Yes, perhaps I'd better bear that in mind."

'Perhaps' was a favourite word of her husband's when he had no intention of obliging. Lina couldn't make up her mind whether or not he was actually worried about the missing women; but it did seem strange, she thought, that both pursued the same career and both had gone missing within a few days of each other.

Chapter Four
ONE FOR THE ROAD

Lina having re-arranged her schedule following their unexpected visit to Yulara, the Binghams now found their free day. It wasn't the one, she decided, on which they wanted to meet Em's family; it was the one they would begin by visiting Miss Olive Pink's Botanical Garden, little more than a stone's throw from their hotel.

Back home, Lina was the gardener. It was she who tended the small, Italianate garden with its low privet hedges, and even cleared the pond at the end of each autumn. Bingham would gaze in admiration as she donned her waders and trod carefully among the water lilies to the consternation of the ducks.

They had decided to breakfast at the garden's Bean Tree Café. Bushfoods were on offer, berries with honey and an oat cereal that Lina enjoyed, while Bing stayed with scrambled eggs on toast washed down with tea that tasted as good as it did back home. Bowerbirds fluttered in and out of the café as they ate, and Bingham wondered, since it was now autumn in Australia, whether mating took place throughout the year.

He tried to keep his mind on the extensive plantings of mulga, eucalyptus and various other tree species: on the arid beauty around the waterhole and the sand dune habitats: on the snakes and goannas signs: on the Red River Gum, whose leaves produced a white, flaky crust that the locals rolled into balls and ate like lollies: on the Grey Cassia, whose hardwood seeds were ground to make biscuit bread. In fact, he was thinking all the time of Helen Lewis and Marjory Fink, both traders of Aboriginal art and both disappearing within a few days of each other. Coincidences were all very well in novels, if only as a means to bring key characters together, but Bingham was sceptical as to how much a part they played in everyday life.

It was over coffee, while he was enjoying a piece of the biscuit bread, that Lina commented on his lack of interest in the garden

"Not at all," he lied, "I was paying close attention."

"Tell me about it, then."

"I was ... eh particularly taken with the native lemon grass. Liquid from its leaves and roots can be crushed and taken in small doses as an aid against the common cold. It can even be massaged into the body."

"Is that true, Bing, or are you just making it up?"

"Perfectly true."

"But that's about all you did notice. Your mind's on those two women, isn't it?"

"Yes. It's something Nellie Doolan said – or didn't say – at Yulara. I can't quite recall the moment, but it will come back to me."

"We'll be there tomorrow."

"Is that the trip you've organised to visit Uluru?"

"Yes. You'll be able to have a chat with Nellie Doolan, then. In the meantime ..."

"... we're on holiday. I know. Sorry, Lina."

"How about driving out to Emily Hawker's place this afternoon? I'd love to see her animals ...," said Lina, adding with a laugh, "and she might remember something else."

Enquiries over lunch at the bar opposite Marjory Fink's gallery and then at the gallery itself, where the young girl held the fort, gave Lina all the information she needed. A phone call to Emily Hawker guaranteed she'd be at home and Lina drove into the animal lover's ramshackle station soon after two o'clock, having driven over terrain dominated by scrub and empty waterholes.

"The station's on a spring," said Emily in answer to Lina's question, "It'd have to be a mighty dry summer for us to run out of water."

Bingham wondered what a 'mighty dry summer' might be like since they were now in autumn and the temperature was topping 43 degrees – a dry, blistering heat obliging even Bingham, who hated them, to wear a hat, the veil of which covered his face and went some way towards keeping the flies at bay.

Emily, a fag end on her lips, was cradling a baby kangaroo, one of those she'd rescued from its mother who she found dead by the roadside. Around her feet or following her like a bridal train were half a dozen cats, bleak-eyed and menacing but seemingly at home with the other animals. Against the wall of the house a water tank, on which a small flock of pigeons enjoyed the shade of the gable end, rested.

A powerful aroma of urine and faeces permeated the whole yard, reminding Bingham of one winter when they brought their children's rabbits and guinea pigs into the house. He'd put his foot down after that occasion and built the creatures a warm wintering place in one of the old outhouses of the farm with bales of straw and an overhead heater.

There was no escaping the smell in Emily's yard, however, and he couldn't see himself wearing the particular pair of desert boots he had on that day ever again.

"Bit of a mess isn't it," Emily said, with a chuckle, and her comment wasn't a question.

Lina and Bingham were given a guided tour of the pens and cages, which seemed to be used more as sleeping quarters than prisons because most of the animals wandered at will: a few goats, three sheep, two pigs, two kangaroos, several possums and, Bingham judged from the droppings, rabbits.

"Are all these rescued animals?" asked Lina.

"Most. Some wander in, of course – especially the rabbits – but I've found most of them injured somewhere or other. They're free to go but they like to stay," replied Emily, her pride and love of her animals clear.

"You look after them alone, do you?"

"No. I've got Alice to help me. She wandered in one day, rather like the beasts, and she's been here ever since. Don't know where she came from or who the hell she is but she's good with the animals. Won't go anywhere else – not even into town – but she seems happy enough. I called her Alice after the town, and she seems to like that. It's good to have a name, don't you think?"

At that moment, an old woman ambled into the yard from around the corner of the house. In her hands she carried a bucket of slops that Bingham judged must be for the pigs. She was fat and unkempt like

Emily but whereas Emily was solidly built Alice's fat was of the sloppy kind and hung from her like loose clothing.

Lina stepped towards her and said hello; Bingham stretched out his hand for a friendly shake. Alice seemed surprised, but took his hand readily enough, while Emily looked on.

After she'd passed by on her way to the sty, Emily said:

"She must have taken to you. It's not everyone who gets a handshake from Alice. Would you like a coffee?"

The kitchen wasn't as bad as Bingham had imagined it might be: it wasn't tidy and the inevitable swarm of desert flies buzzed around a stack of unwashed dishes and plates of food that had been left on the draining board, but it was free from droppings and the awful smell of urine, provided you took a seat away from the open window, and Emily took clean cups from a wall cupboard and drew fresh water from a tap.

The coffee was good, strong and black but with an underlying sweetness. In the corner of the kitchen, a television set rolled out endless news, most of it local: a local councillor fearing her chances of re-selection, bush cops building up huge leave balances because their numbers were inadequate, kangaroo balls falling from the sky, a car torched and a youth arrested, the Queen's baton welcomed with traditional dancing at Uluru National Park, local art gallery owner missing …

"I've seen her!"

Alice stood in the doorway, reaching out for the cup of coffee Emily handed her and watching the television.

"Seen who, Alice?" asked Emily, who was neither listening to nor watching the news.

"Her on the box," replied Alice, pointing at the screen. Marjory Fink's firm face filled the television.

"When was this?" asked Bingham.

"Yesterday morning. She was out by the ranges. She was in her car."

"Did she speak?" asked Bingham.

"Didn't see me. She came from …"

"Came from where, Alice," asked Emily, her eyes fixed on the other woman.

"I don't know – near here, I think … it was this way …," replied Alice, pointing frantically and leaving in what Bingham thought was a hurried manner, gripping her coffee cup.

"You have a place in town, don't you?" Bingham asked Emily.

"That's right."

"And that's where you found the note?"

"Yes – I said."

"I wonder why she didn't call in if she was passing this way. She could then have asked you to look after the gallery rather than leaving a note … And why didn't she leave the note here?"

"Beats me. Maybe she was in a hurry."

"What would Alice have been doing out by the ranges?"

"Bush tucker. She collects some most mornings."

"She wasn't ill in any way, was she?"

"I told you, George – stop worrying. Marje's OK!"

"Apart from you, who were her friends?"

"Everyone. Everyone loved Marje."

"Any particular one?"

"You mean a bloke?"

"No – I was thinking more of a woman friend."

"There was Sarah. She bought a load of art stuff from Marje when she settled down here, and they became mates. She was a doctor at the Alice Springs Hospital until she retired. Lives this side of the river – Kurrajong Drive – nice area. What they call 'sought after'. Not like my place. You'll pass by her place on the way back. Call in. Say hello."

Lina was both fascinated by the idea of calling on a complete stranger and dubious about their reception, and so she tried to persuade Bingham to do no such thing, while at the same time hoping he would take the chance.

Bingham was naturally reticent, but this English affliction had faded over the past three years, ever since his search for Natalie Beddoes had plunged him, head first, into a new world. Somewhere at the back of his mind was a remark Nellie Doolan had made (was it a remark or something she hadn't said?) and now there was Alice's hurried exit and the unfinished 'this way' accompanied by the pointing finger. There was also his tenacity: a quality his mother had described as 'being like a dog with a bone'.

"Are you sure, Bing?" was Lina's last comment when they drew up outside *Dreamtime* on Kurrajong Drive.

The house was the "nature lover's dream" Emily had shouted to them as she waved goodbye. It overlooked the bush and had a walking and biking track on the doorstep. Brick and clearly privately built the house stood in its own grounds.

"What are you going to say, Bing?"

"I wasn't sure but I know now. I won't be a moment."

With that remark, Bingham climbed out of their hired vehicle and wandered aimlessly around as though he'd lost his way. He peered into the garden of the house and looked around as though seeking a path that might lead behind the property. He did this for a while, pushing alongside *Dreamtime* and returning to the road several times, while Lina watched from the car. He rubbed his head, returned to the car for a brochure and stood puzzling over it.

Eventually, a woman came from the house, a broad smile on her face.

"Are you lost?"

The voice was cultured. She was obviously a woman in her sixties but could, in a favourable light, have passed for forty-something such was the trimness of her figure and the glow of health radiating from her tanned face.

"My wife and I were looking for a walk that would take us down to the river. There's a circular one somewhere here, I believe."

"It's a fair distance. You'd be better off starting out in the cool of the morning and stopping off at the telegraph station on your way. It's not a walk to be hurried. I'm Sarah Eastman, by the way."

"George – George Bingham and my wife …"

Bingham paused as he waited for Lina to come over from the car.

"… Lina. As you might guess, we're on holiday."

"Nice to meet you. Come in and have a drink. You look as though you could do with one. Thirty-five degrees is considered hot enough around here. This present temperature is unbelievable. Where are you folks from?"

"We live in a little village to the north of Ipswich in East Anglia," said Lina, "Our house is what was a farmhouse. It belonged to my parents."

"I know East Anglia: beautiful countryside and wide-open skies. I trained in Cambridge but got itchy feet and came out here more years ago than I care to remember. It's a shame my husband isn't here. He'd love to meet you."

"Is your husband local?"

"Local enough – Adelaide," replied Sarah Eastman with a laugh.

"You say that you trained in Cambridge," asked Bingham.

"I'm a doctor – or I was. I retired a few years ago."

"And your husband ...?" asked Lina, leaving the question in the air.

"Stan's in finance – real estate. We met through his rumbling appendix – four children ago! Come on in. Let's get you that drink."

"It's very kind of you," said Lina, "What a lovely house."

Bingham followed the two women, content to leave the chatter to Lina. She was good at conversation, and it would take time to bring the subject round to the missing art dealer.

He loved places and houses fell into that category. This one, *Dreamtime* – and they'd come to that name, later – had, obviously, been looked after, meticulously. It was a house you could enjoy.

Sarah guided them through sliding glass doors to an outdoor living area where she sat them in the shade of a tree and under a sail before placing two large beers before them. Bingham admired the view, while Lina and Sarah talked. He reflected on how fortunate they were that this was Australia and that they were among Australians. Back home – he smiled as he thought the phrase that was becoming second nature to him now – they would not so readily have been welcomed into a stranger's home.

His welcome usually depended on the fact that he was looking for a missing person and upon whether or not the person he approached was willing to help. Here, in the Red Centre, he wasn't looking for anybody. Bingham had to keep reminding himself of the actual truth: he was simply on holiday.

A second beer and several Anzac biscuits later, Bingham heard Lina mention their purchase at the arts gallery. He waited: it was better that Sarah should be the first to speak Marjory Fink's name, and she did.

"I know Marje well. Stan – that's my husband - and I bought our soft furnishings through Marje. Bit of a character, of course. What you'd call a rough diamond back home. She seems to have gone AWOL for a bit."

"We met her on our first night here," said Bingham, "and were there the next morning when the police officer was making his enquiries. The general feeling is that she's gone walkabout ... "

He left the phrase hanging, hoping a pause might provoke a continuation. It did.

"Marje isn't the sort to go walkabout. I like her and I think she's fair with the Aboriginals who produce the crafts she sells, but there's nothing mystical about Marje. You say you've met her, and so you'll know what I mean."

"Down to earth?" suggested Bingham.

"And earthy," added Sarah with a smile, "With Marje, what you see is what you get – and you don't see an abstract interest in the Aboriginals culture, do you?"

"No, I suppose you don't," replied Bingham, eager for Sarah to continue, desperate not to appear eager.

As the conversation hung in the balance, he looked her over again. Her trimness was accentuated by the slim-line trousers she wore and the loose top held in gently at the waist by a plaited, leather belt that looked as though it had come from the gallery. Her hair was a natural colour, blonde and shoulder length, free but cut by someone who knew their job.

Bingham wondered about her relationship with Marjory Fink. She spoke fondly of her and respected her nature, but did they socialise? Or was he being so English by even thinking that they might not? This was a young country, full of hope. Did the traditional barriers exist, as at home?

"We met another friend of hers at the gallery," said Lina, suddenly, as though to bring the others out of their reverie, "Emily Hawker. She was helping out. It was she who sold us the didgeridoo."

"Oh, Em," laughed Sarah, "Now those two do look like peas in a pod."

"We were out at her place earlier today," said Bingham, pursuing the strand that might lead back to Marjory Fink, "She invited us to see her animals."

"Her family, you mean! She's a wonderful woman. All right – sloppy and smelly: but with a heart of gold. She spends all her money on those creatures she rescues, you know."

"You say that you don't think Marje has gone on a Dreamtime journey?" asked Bingham.

"It wouldn't be Marje."

"Alice thought she may have seen her driving towards the MacDonnell Ranges."

"You met Alice as well! You get to know the local characters, George."

"Emily didn't seem to know who she was …"

"… or where she came from. I know. Alice is as near as anyone gets to being an animal while still appearing human. I don't mean that in any derogatory sense, by the way. Animals play a large part in Aboriginal culture. Walek, the frill-necked lizard, brought the people of Nelgi Island the gift of fire; the egg of the great bird, Brolga, gave us the sun; Snake cuts out the river beds and brings us water – you get the drift! Alice is in touch with all those things. It brings compassion to her dealings with the animals."

"You think she may be part Aboriginal?"

"Who knows? It's a hard world out there. I'm just pleased she found Em … Although, you never know with the Aboriginals. One day, she might be up and off."

"You obviously have a respect for their beliefs," said Lina.

"I try to understand them but just when I'm getting close my understanding takes two steps back. They're a strange people. We saw the rough side of their life in the hospital …"

Sarah Eastman paused for a moment – wondering whether or not to continue, thought Bingham – and then went on:

"… rough side from our point of view, that is. The men have these initiation rites. They go off to one of their sacred rocks – the Olgas is one place mentioned – and the young men are circumcised, and it isn't done under surgical conditions! The urethra is also cut and the body is scarred. They call it 'men's business', and the women just *do not* get involved. I know how I'd feel if it was a son of mine going through it!

"We also came across the punishments they inflict on each other if they believe one of them is responsible for another's death. The traditional sentence is a spear through the leg or a clubbing. We experienced horrific wounds at the hospital."

"So, they do come for help" asked Lina.

"They would die if they didn't. It's a wonder some of those young men didn't bleed to death on the way."

Bingham closed off as the two women continued talking. He'd hoped that something Sarah might say would give them an inkling as to why Marjory Fink had decided to wander off. Not that it was any of his business, but he didn't like the idea of a woman roaming around the Outback alone.

"What was Marje's view of these things?" he asked eventually.

"As I said, she isn't the mystical sort. 'Take it or leave it' would be her attitude. She had a good business relationship with them. What they did in their spare time was nothing to do with her."

"So why do you think she's wandered off?"

"Your guess is as good as mine, George. I admit it seems a bit sudden but there may be people she knows out there. Tennant Creek is that way on. You seem fixed on the idea that she's gone walkabout. Why?"

"We were in Yulara a few days ago," said Lina, "and a lady who ran an art gallery there has also gone missing – suddenly, like Marje," adding with a smile, "and George thinks coincidences should be confined to novels."

"Would that be Helen Lewis?"

"You know her?"

"Not as well as we know Marje, obviously, but we took a trip down there when we were looking for furnishings for this place. She's a different kettle of fish to Marje: very refined, as I remember. She buys from the locals, doesn't she? It's the Anangu people there, isn't it? I'd no idea she'd gone missing. What makes you think that?"

"We saw a notice asking for information about her in both the Mt Ebenezer Roadhouse and the Stuart's Well one," replied Lina.

"A police notice?"

"It had their number but looked homemade," answered Bingham, "It occurred to us that someone was concerned, and then we arrive here and the very day we do Marje leaves without warning. Do you know anything about her son? We met him at the gallery."

"'Least said, soonest mended' as far as he's concerned: bad marriage, bad blood, bad just about everything. Stan and I never met Marje's husband. According to Em, we are the lucky ones."

"Is he still alive?"

"No – a lucky accident for everyone, except the kangaroo he hit, when he went off the road. Broke his neck. Marje threw a party. The son's never forgiven her."

"That must be upsetting for her?" said Lina.

"I don't think so. She thinks he'll come round one day but if he doesn't she isn't going to lose any sleep over it. What you can't change you accept is her motto. Marje does all right. She never alone, you might say ... Look, Stan'll be back in a while. Would you folks like to have a meal with us?"

Knowing that Lina wouldn't like to refuse, and knowing that he and she liked time alone, Bingham said, quickly:

"Thanks for the offer, Sarah, but we've promised another couple at Double Trees that we'll eat with them this evening. We're on the same trip tomorrow and we wouldn't want to cause any offence."

"Course not – I understand – but if you get the chance to drop in again, please do. I've enjoyed the chat. You're off to Uluru, are you? You'll enjoy the experience."

"What couple are we sharing a meal with this evening, Bing?" Lina asked as they drove back into Alice.

"It was only a white lie, Lina – one that avoided causing offence."

"There was no need to embroider it with 'we're all on the same trip tomorrow'."

"It added credibility. I know you don't like lies of any sort but that one hurt nobody."

"It's the principle that matters."

"It's what remains in you of a guilty conscious brought about by a Catholic upbringing."

"You liked my mother."

"I loved your mother, but that isn't what we're talking about."

"We're talking about the way she brought me up – never to lie."

"And quite right, too."

"What if Sarah and her husband find us eating alone in Alice tonight?"

"Leave it to me."

"Anyway, it's not tomorrow we're going to Uluru. It's the day after."

Bingham smiled. They'd had this conversation many times and he knew Lina would have the last word – she always did – but it brought them back laughing to Alice and they ate, that night, once again, in the Hanuman bar, Lina enjoying a kofta curry and Bingham a dish of seasonal mixed vegetables.

Buoyed up by their feelings for each other and talking about their trip that Lina had arranged, they wandered once more into Alice Springs. Their nightly walks had taken on a pattern, however unconsciously. They would walk from their hotel, crossing the dried-up bed of the Todd via the Tuncks Road Bridge. They would then re-trace their steps on the other side of the riverbed, walk past the hospital (on this night more meaningful to them, having met Sarah Eastman), cross by the sports ground and then double back into the centre, where they would find themselves in the outdoor precinct containing Marjory Fink's art gallery and the bar where they felt at home.

As usual, they passed groups of Aboriginals talking together around a scattering of bottles of wine and beer on the riverbank or by the sports park. Lina couldn't help commenting – after they'd passed by – how poorly dressed the people were and wondering why, if it was true the government was doling out money right, left and centre. As they passed, someone in the group would call out to them. The call always sounded like a series of 'g-days, but Bingham was unsure. Once or twice one of them had stood and staggered towards him and Lina but had got no further than an outstretched arm and a wave.

On this evening they found the gallery open with the lights on. A truck was parked in front of the shop and the man they took to be the driver was climbing off the back. The young girl who worked in the gallery was standing at the side of the road talking to him. He lifted several boxes from the truck and placed them by her feet. The night was hot and Bingham noticed the man was sweating profusely as he and Lina approached. Despite the relative cool of the evening, the flies were everywhere, crawling in the perspiration that ran from the man's hair and from around his eyes.

"Murdoch Hill Chardonnay," said Bingham, "$25 a bottle if you buy it from the regular retailers, and a nice drop of plonk."

A none-too-friendly look on his already grizzled face, the man turned to Bingham. He was a lean man, a man whose strength existed not so much in muscle bulk as in his sinews, Bingham thought. His mass of hair, though drenched in sweat, was cut tidily and the black work boots were polished to a high shine. He wore an open-necked shirt over a t-shirt, the sleeves of which were folded back partway to his elbows, and a pair of expensive jeans.

"We had a drink with Marje the other night," explained Lina, quickly, "'always got a drink on hand in the gallery – softens folks up' she said."

"Oh, right, Marje. You know Marje."

"She told us the wine came from the Adelaide Hills and said a friend dropped some off for her once in a while," continued Lina

"Too true."

"Has there been any news of her yet?" asked Bingham.

"No, no there hasn't. It's a bit of a worry."

"Can I give you a hand with those cases of wine," asked Bingham, lifting one from the ground without waiting for an answer and walking into the gallery, where the girl opened the door of the back office for him.

"Down there," she said.

"I do apologise," said Bingham to the girl, "We haven't actually met, have we?" I'm George and my wife is Lina. Thanks for wrapping the didgeridoo for us so carefully."

"It's a pleasure. "Katy – that's me."

"And a nice little lady, too. Thanks for opening up. I'm Bob, by the way. Pleased to meet you," said the trucker, turning to George and Lina and shaking their hands.

"You didn't know Marje had gone?" asked Bingham.

"No. I phoned Katy here when I got no answer from Marje. Didn't want to leave the plonk with just anyone, although I suppose Reg over the road at the cafe would have looked after it for me at a push."

"You do this trip regularly, do you?"

"Back and forth all the time."

"It must be tiring. You'll want to get your head down," said Lina.

"I'll have a couple of beers before I do. Helps me get to sleep."

"Can we buy you one?" asked Bingham, "We're about to have a drink ourselves."

"Well, that's decent of you. I'll just get these last cases in and then ..."

Bob left his sentence unfinished while he and Bingham lifted the remaining cases of wine into the office and Katy locked the gallery. It was only when they were sitting in the bar that he continued more or less where he'd left off.

"I don't drink or sleep on the way. You get used to it. I might spend twenty minutes here and there with my eyes closed, but that's all. The cab's air-conditioned. I see to that. I wouldn't take out a truck that wasn't. You see these drivers sitting in lay-bys, the sweat pouring from them, dosing their heads with bottles. Some of these companies aren't bothered, but I don't drive for them – no way."

"We saw some of the signs on the way up here," said Bingham, "'Stop, Rest, Survive', 'Fatigue kills' – that sort of thing."

"The police'll pull you over if they see you wobbling or think you're on the amphetamines to keep you awake, but I never touch the bloody things. Mind you, the reality is that you have to deliver on time and that isn't easy when you're covering thousands of miles across the outback for a drop off."

"You do the whole run, do you – Adelaide to Darwin?"

"Too right. Adelaide to Darwin and all points in between. You name them. I've been there – Coober Pedy, Tennant Creek, Yulara, Katherine. Anywhere along the Stuart and a hundred miles or so on either side of it. I'm off troppo tomorrow."

"What do you carry?"

"Fruit and veg, mainly – papayas, pineapples, passion fruits, bananas, mangoes from up the top end and apples, blackberries, cherries, plums and peaches from down south."

Several beers later, Lina and Bingham parted company with Bob Evans – they'd eventually learned his last name when the talk drifted 'back home' and he mentioned his family had come out from Wales in the 1950s on a £10 ticket - but they'd learned nothing more about Marje than they knew already; the missing woman seemed as far away as ever.

Chapter Five
SIMPSONS GAP

The following day had been carefully planned by Lina. It was to be their last one with the Holden that had brought them from Adelaide; on the morrow, they would be off on the coach tour to Uluru and the Kata Tjuta National Park and the Holden would be picked up and driven on to its next customer.

Meanwhile, there was the Desert Park, Flynn's Grave, Simpsons Gap and Standley Chasm – museums, cultural sites, habitat walks, spectacular scenery and wildlife – to visit, if they held out in the heat.

It was at Simpsons Gap, about sixteen miles from Alice, where they met the young woman. The site had the usual tourist information and picnic tables and offered what were described as 'interpretive walks'. Both Bingham and Lina enjoyed walking and decided to attempt one at an easy fitness level after a black coffee in Bingham's case and a cool drink in Lina's. The young woman was sitting at one of the picnic benches, a banner proclaiming SORRY BOOK tacked to the table.

While Bingham bought the drinks, Lina wandered over, curious about the notice and thinking about Marjory Fink, who according to Alice must have made off in this direction.

The young woman smiled up at her and Lina looked at the book on the table. She'd guessed its purpose: an apology to the original natives of Australia for the way they'd been treated by the first settlers and a wish that the future might treat them better. Lina looked at the young woman, wondering whether to sign; after all, she was only a holidaymaker and pointless gestures were not in her nature. She said so.

"I'm Yvonne," said the young woman, "one of the lost generation to which the book refers. Your signing it is anything but an empty gesture: it's a sign of solidarity."

"I'm Lina," she replied, "I'm pleased to meet you."

She took the outstretched hand and noticed for the first time that Yvonne was a light, natural brown, not coloured by the sun but by her ancestry.

"What's the lost generation," she asked, eager to know more.

"Do you know anything of my country's history?"

"A little, but through reading and visits to your museums: that's not the same as hearing someone's personal account. May I sit down?"

Yvonne gestured to a chair at the side of the table.

"Many of us – and I was one – were taken from our mothers at birth. We were given all sorts of reasons but the real one was that the authorities wanted to assimilate us into white society. There was a belief that the blackness could be bred out of us. We were used as servants. Some of us were lucky: we ended up in families. Others of us were not. Many were worked into the ground on the sheep stations. Many were abused – sometimes by the Catholic priests at the missions.

"This book is a start. We are not interested in compensation; we are interested in those who abused us being called to account. We are interested in justice being done. All the money in the world cannot hide what has happened."

"You ended up with a good family?"

Yvonne, her eyes flashing with anger, looked at Lina before answering.

"You can tell I am educated?"

"Yes."

"It was a good family, but it was not my family."

"No, of course not, I understand."

"Family is important to my people. When we children were taken, it removed the heart from our culture."

"Have you never found your mother?"

"I am still searching. She disappeared like so many others – and, despite what you say, you do not understand."

"No, it was silly of me to say so."

"Have you come from Alice?"

"Yes."

"You've seen those down at the river?"

"Yes."

"They are the lost ones, also. The clans around here are travellers. We move around because it is in our genes to do so. For tens of thousands of years, we have been hunters and gatherers. That is how we lived and now, our way of life is taken from us. We cannot remain in one place for long."

"But there are those of your people who do …"

"… to provide *arts and crafts* for the tourists!"

Yvonne almost spat out the charge.

"The ones we've met did not seem angry at the idea."

"What else is there for them? And you are wrong. We move around, we meet, we talk, we share news, we visit relatives but we do not stay long in one place. It is not natural."

"Are you from here? Is this where you were a servant?"

"No. It is from here I was taken to Melbourne."

"You say you have never found your mother, but your father ...?"

Lina left the question hanging, feeling the young woman did not want to acknowledge her father.

"You are right," she replied, "My father was white."

"And you feel that you belong to neither culture and that neither culture offers you a home?"

"I have no sense of belonging."

"And what of the whites who try to understand your culture?"

"They are walking in the dark."

The young woman looked away. Their conversation at an end, Lina signed the book. It seemed the polite thing to do. She hadn't meant to stir the proverbial hornets' nest. She hadn't expected such anger. Once again, so near to the question she wanted to ask, the chance had been snatched away.

"I don't believe these people have anything to do with the disappearance of either Helen Lewis or Marjory Fink, whatever anger many of them might feel," said Bingham, when Lina, glancing through one of the brochures Bingham had picked up at the tourist information desk, had relayed her conversation with Yvonne. "I do believe that Helen may have gone Walkabout – if that's the right word – but I doubt the same is true of Marjory."

"It's just a coincidence, then?"

"Coincidences are for Russian novels," replied Bingham with a smile, "Isn't this a beautiful place?"

"Don't change the subject, Bing. Don't cut me out from what you're thinking."

"I'm not, Lina – not really. I'm just trying to remember that we're on holiday. This is a beauty spot, a spiritual refuge for the Arrernte people," he replied, "and ..." he added with a smile, since he knew his wife's desire to see one in the wild, "the home of the black-footed rock wallaby."

Lina laughed. She knew her husband's ways.

"It must have offered a real refuge at one time," she said, "I suppose it still does in some ways. It's cooler than the surrounding desert, sheltered by these craggy, red slopes and look at the waterhole. Let's go, Bing. Let's walk. According to this brochure, it's a place where Dreaming trails and stories cross."

Simpsons Gap was their last excursion that day. Beautiful though the country was, the heat had overcome them by the time they returned to their car. Only in the cover of the red cliffs was it possible to find shade: elsewhere they traversed strips of sand obstructed by huge boulders of the quartzite. They were scorched – Bingham, laughingly, suggested fried, such was the oily nature of the sweat that dripped from them – and besieged by the inevitable flies.

Alone, Lina thought, they would have been frightened. Even in the relative cool of the chasm, she was aware of the desert that lay beyond, an area of shrivelled bushes and the spiny-leaved grasses that formed tussocks in the sand. Her admiration for the people who made their lives here increased; she could only wonder at their daily struggle and, yet again, her thoughts returned to Helen Lewis and Marjory Fink.

In the gap, itself, they came across the acacias, the shrubs and trees with their grey foliage that form a dense scrubby growth, the gum trees – the ghosts and the river reds – and the lemon grasses that seemed to survive anywhere. But even there, shuttered from the sun, the flies found them and they returned to their vehicle veiled and in need of a drink.

Bingham's comment about coincidence wasn't, Lina thought, to be taken too seriously (her husband was well-known for making remarks for which he had no regard) and when they returned early to Alice Springs and found themselves – Bingham liked the idea of finding a place rather than seeking it out – drinking a well-earned beer in Reg's Bar, they witnessed an altercation outside the gallery opposite that was to prove fruitful.

Henry Fink stood in front of his mother's gallery arguing with a young woman. It was obvious from the way they stood that they were not strangers to each other: intimate but at odds was the observation Bingham made to Lina. Watching the young woman, Bingham knew he had to speak with her.

"But how, Bing? You can't just walk up to her."

"No. You're a woman, Lina. Think of something. We can't let her get away. That young man worried me ... Drink up."

Seeing them approach, Henry Fink's anger spread; one moment he was shouting at the young woman, the next, glaring at Bingham and Lina. The cuff fiddling, the head lowering and the pushing of his glasses to the bridge of the nose seemed only to exaggerate his unpleasant mood. Adopting his mildest tone, one calculated to induce anger in the most unassuming person when their emotions were grazed and certain to succeed with Henry, Bingham said:

"Can we help?"

"You can fuck off."

"Don't spit the dummy, Henry," said the young woman, laughing and drawing Bingham and Lina into her riposte.

For a moment, Bingham thought that Henry was going to strike his girlfriend but the moment passed in a flurry of cuff arranging and glasses adjusting before he turned and stormed off out of the little precinct.

"Hi," said the young woman, "I'm Fern. Sorry about Henry. He's having a bad day."

"George ... uhm, and my wife, Lina. We met Henry's mother a few days ago."

"Don't worry about Henry," replied Fern, sensing what she took to be Bingham's embarrassment, "He'll get over it. Please to meet you."

"What did you mean by 'spit the dummy'?" asked Bingham.

"Like a baby, wasn't he, having a tantrum?"

"Is he often like that?" asked Lina.

"Comes and goes."

"You don't seem too bothered."

"I'm more worried about his mum. Henry, I can take or leave but I like Marje. She used to give me work when I got back from university. It helped me through the summer."

"Is that where you met Henry?"

"God, no! I've known him from school."

"Just good friends?" suggested Lina.

"Bit more than that," replied Fern, with a laugh, "if you know what I mean."

"Why are you worried about Marje?"

"It's not like her to wander off without warning. It's not like her to wander off at all! She's a social person – fun-loving. She likes people around her."

"Yes, that's how she struck us. We met a friend of hers last night – was it last night?"

"Time gets distorted when you're on holiday," said Fern, her infectious laugh going with the remark, "You mean Bob Evans. Oh, they're *very* good friends."

"He seemed worried, too. Is that what's upsetting Henry?"

"No, he's got a hangover from the drinking game last night. Things didn't quite turn out as he expected." As she spoke, Fern winked at Lina as though they shared a secret known only among women. "I don't want to hold you folks up," she continued, "You're on holiday. Go, enjoy yourselves. I'll find Henry and calm him down."

With a wave, she was gone in the direction of Todd Mall.

"What were they arguing about, do you think?" Bingham asked Lina.

"Who knows? For some people, it's a way of life. But let's 'go, enjoy ourselves'... She was nicely dressed, wasn't she, Bing?"

"Pardon? Yes. Yes she was," replied Bingham, amazed at how Lina switched thoughts partway through a conversation, amazed despite having experienced it all his life among nearly all the women he had known at work and at home. But Lina was right: Fern had been well turned out: a light summery dress, discreetly cut, her sandals clean despite the dust, her long blonde hair tied back in pony tail, a straw hat perched neatly on the crown of her head. Quite old-fashioned in her dress, and yet not in her attitudes, thought Bingham.

"I expect she's at work," he said.

"And they'd met up during one of her breaks?"

"I suppose so."

"What are you thinking?"

Once again, that irritating question: Bingham wasn't sure what he was thinking, but something had struck home, something Fern had said. If only he could remember. And the young man, Henry: did he know more than he was saying? What had the young couple been arguing about so heatedly?

Tomorrow, they'd be off to Yulara on Lina's trip to the sacred rock: a two-day excursion with *Outback Tours*. Maybe they'd have a chance to speak with Nellie Doolan again – no, not 'maybe', definitely. Nellie had said something, too, that had caught his attention. If only, he could remember.

Chapter Six

ROADHOUSE

The Stuart Highway stretched before them once again. This time from an air-conditioned coach and with an excellent guide, but it lacked the spontaneity, the chance encounters they'd experienced driving their own vehicle. Time would be limited at each stop: time to wander and talk, time to ask questions, time to wonder.

Bingham had experienced one of his restless nights. Back home (he was getting used to the phrase now) he would have crept from their bed to the kitchen, made a cup of tea, hushed the dogs as he passed through the cloakroom to his study and then tossed and turned on the settee he used when he didn't want to wake Lina. He might even have meandered down to the orchard if he could have left the house without disturbing the dogs. It was at times such as those – when he was alone in the world, undistracted by any other concern – that those stray memories returned. It might only be a phrase he was searching for, perhaps something as simple as a gesture or an odd word, but he could haul it in, bring it to shore and make his catch.

At their hotel, all he had been able to do was sit and stare from the window. He'd been withdrawn during breakfast at Picccolo's Café and Lina, sensing his abstraction, had enjoyed her croissant and coffee in silence. Afterwards, waiting for the coach, she'd asked:

"Have you found what you're looking for?"

"No, Lina, nothing has occurred to me. Let's enjoy the day."

But Bingham had been looking forward as well as back and at the Stuarts Well Roadhouse where they stopped for coffee or – in most cases – a cool drink, his anticipation was rewarded: memories had been stirred following their first visit.

It was Lina who received the first foretaste of what was to come. While Bingham sat in the heat under one of the original Coca-Cola signs enticing two yellow-billed birds with what fell from his flapjack, she wandered over to the pens where the animals were kept. On their first visit, she'd made the acquaintance of one of the keepers, and Lina was nothing if not sociable. The man's name was Ted and he'd allowed her to feed one of the young kangaroos. Lina had not forgotten the soft feel of the animal's mouth as it nuzzled her hand for food.

"Good to see you again. Off to Ayers Rock are you?"

"Yes, our time here's nearly over. When we return to Alice in two days' time, we're off to Cairns."

"Great place Cairns – wide streets. Take a walk down to the marina and look out for the fruit bats. There's a little copse of trees right in the middle of the main street. That's where you'll find the bats. Do you want to feed the little fella?"

"Love to."

Ted handed her a fistful of various grains that Lina held out to the young animal and once again felt its gentle mouthing against her palm.

"When you were here last they tell me you were asking about the missing woman poster. Is that right?"

"Yes, we met the lady's cleaner in Yulara. She seemed disturbed by Helen's disappearance."

"Never saw the lady myself – not here – wasn't one of her places. But I know who asked the boss to put the poster up. It was a friend of hers – one of the truckers. A bloke called Bob Evans. He drops off fruit and veg – that kind of thing. He's a regular on the Stuart. Nice bloke."

Lina laughed so much she almost disturbed the kangaroo feeding.

"What's so funny?"

"We met Mr Evans only the other night. It never occurred to either of us to ask about Helen. Why would it? Wait 'til I tell Bing. Thank you for letting me feed the kangaroo. I must get back. We've only a short time here. Perhaps we'll meet again on the way back to Alice."

"I hope so, lady – nice to make your acquaintance."

Lina was still chuckling when she sat across the table from Bingham and passed on her news.

"We had no reason to suppose that Mr Evans knew both ladies," he said.

"It does strike you as odd, though, doesn't it, Bing?"

"Yes, it does, especially as there's no missing person poster of Marjory Fink at the bar. If it was Bob Evans who put up the first poster – and we've only your friend's memory to serve us on that point …"

"… He did seem certain, Bing. They'd obviously talked about it."

"… why hasn't he put up a second poster? Surely, he'd be as interested in finding one of the women as he would in finding the other. He's clearly worried about Helen ..."

"... He hasn't had a chance, Bing. He was on his way north to Darwin."

"Oh, of course – yes – I remember – 'off troppo' was the expression, wasn't it?"

Yes, he remembered – just! Of course, Bob Evans had had no chance of putting up a poster of Marjory Fink: he was travelling north. At the age of seventy-four, Bingham was aware he was forgetting too much. He'd remember a film they'd enjoyed and would recall the name of a leading actor – the first name, that is. It might be in the early hours two days later that the surname came to him. Not Alzheimer's – not yet, please God: a slip of memory can happen to anyone at any age.

"Do you know where the toilets are, Bing? I've forgotten."

"Out back," he replied, with a laugh, "Corrugated metal affairs. The 'gents' has a camel's head on the sign.

"Excuse me a moment. I must go before we go."

The heat had settled in by now, making Bingham uncomfortable even in the shade of the veranda as it bounced off the metal walls behind him. There were, thank God, no flies as yet. Perhaps they didn't like the shade, he thought as he rose from the plastic chair and went to look for the dog the notice told him not to touch or feed.

He was chatting amiably to the animal, which was eyeing him warily, when Lina returned. He knew at once that she had something on her mind and he waited. Nothing came. It was unlike Lina not to open up at once – she was an open book as far as her thoughts were concerned – but Bingham said nothing. He had sensed that this roadhouse offered a key of some kind to what might – or, again, might not – be a mystery. People's memories were often stirred by subsequent events. Time – they needed time here, and the tour guide had offered twenty minutes.

Back on the coach, Lina whispered in his ear:

"I had a conversation with someone in the ladies".

"There's no point in whispering, Lina. I'm partially deaf – remember?"

"I can't say it out loud."

"Let's wait until we get to our lunch stop, then."

"The Stuart is the lifeline of our country," said the tour guide. "It carries goods and people from Darwin in the north to Adelaide in the south and – beyond. The roadhouses – and Stuarts Well is one of the greatest – pump adrenalin into the system – as well as gas and booze. There's nowhere else to stop and so you tend to see the same faces again and again if you make the trip as often as I do. There's always someone you've met before, always someone to share a drink and a bit of gossip. There's nothing like a roadhouse to supply a bit of gossip …"

Bingham, half-listening, couldn't help but wish they'd been provided with a little more.

"Of course, we don't drink on the job – if you'll excuse the expression – but that's not always true with the truckers. They say that beer oils the works – keeps them alert. No worries. Australians don't drink like those of you from Europe or America. You drink with your meals, don't you? We drink at any time of the day. It's bad form not to offer someone a drink when you meet up and no one ever skips their round. That's social isolation for you …"

Bingham thought of the French workers he'd seen knocking back a brandy on their way to work in the morning. Never trust stereotypes, he thought, and smiled at Lina.

The tour guide was a paean of enlightenment; his knowledge inexhaustible, he seemed to know the name of every tree and every creature along the Stuart and his tales of the odd and eccentric kept the tourists laughing and nodding sagely. His tale of the Outback Ranger who had descended twenty-eight feet into a dunny to retrieve the watch of a Japanese tourist for a reward of £5000 was, perhaps, the highlight of their journey. It certainly brought the party to a stop at a modern dunny, an immaculate corrugated iron structure, approached by a wooden ramp from the side of the road. It wasn't elegant but it was functional, serving the needs of those who'd forgotten to go at the roadhouse. While the party queued (there was only one cubicle for each sex), Lina relayed what Bingham had been unable to hear above the sound of the coach.

"I was in the toilet at the roadhouse and one of the staff who was in there spoke to me. She said that they'd all been talking after we left on the way to Alice Springs and remembered that Helen Lewis has called in one day ..."

"Going where?"

"Bing!"

"Sorry – go on."

"They thought she was going to Alice. Anyway, there was a man at the bar – obviously drunk – and he was sounding off about the Aboriginal people. You know the kind of thing: they're lazy buggers, drunk most of the time, never turn up for a job even when they've got one and live on government handouts. Well, Helen took exception to this and challenged him.

"She began explaining that their land and their way of life had been taken from them with no 'by your leave', that they'd faced a policy of extermination, hunted down like animals, that they were a creative people and Australia's tourist industry depended on their artistry.

"The man – a great bully of a man – turned on her, called her a 'fucking smart arse' and a 'fucking whore', and said she thought she was 'too fucking good for them'."

Lina dropped her voice to an inaudible whisper on the swear words and the body parts, but Bingham picked out 'good for them'.

"Can you just speak up a bit, Lina?"

"I can't. There are people around … The woman said his eyes were bloodshot and the veins stood out on his forehead. He came over to her table and towered above her. He was obviously wound up. He was clenching and unclenching his fists as though he was going to hit her, when the barman stepped in and told him he'd had enough. The man then turned on the barman and said he 'could drink himself sober'.

"It was an ugly scene, Bing, but Helen Lewis never lost her cool, even when the yelling started. She remained at her table and finished her coffee."

"Quite the lady isn't she," Bingham commented, "I wonder what she was doing at the Stuart Wells. She buys her crafts from the Imanpa people."

"People do travel, Bing. She might have been having a day out in Alice Springs."

"I suppose so."

All along, Bingham had felt he knew Helen Lewis: her home, the painting on her wall, her dealings with her craftspeople, her gallery and her husband's death. Now, her attitude confirmed those feelings. She was considered and considerate. She was not the kind of person to wander off without a word to those she knew.

His mind was settled and he relaxed. The bottom line was drawn. Bingham liked bottom lines; uncertainty was what troubled him.

As the coach set off again, everyone relieved, he sat back in his seat and dozed. He'd had a restless night. A cat nap was all he needed and then he'd wake and enjoy the journey.

He wasn't sure when he woke or whether he'd slept at all. His head was a mind full of information from somewhere – his own reading or the tour guide's voice – but survival was the keyword; the desert oak, its massive roots digging deep into the water table, its foliage burnt but the tree, itself, still living; the tough acacias they'd come across at Simpson's Gap with their flattened, silvery leaves that reflected the heat; the small but spectacular flowers of the desert, full of the nectar that fed so many insects and the honey-eaters; the spiny leaves of the tjanpi, cooling the sand for the animals, providing food for grazing mammals, seeds for the artist and a focus for the Dreaming.

Threading through his own dreaming, there was Lina's voice 'there comes a time in a woman's life when she has to decide her destiny ... the overall journey ... for some, it comes naturally but for others it's brought about by a shock'.

"Bing, wake up. We're almost there."

"Yulara? We can't be ..."

"No – the Mt Ebenezer Roadhouse. I didn't like to wake you. You've been asleep for over an hour."

It was always like that nowadays. At one time, a twenty-minute catnap was all he needed but not now, as an old man. Bingham woke again as they turned off the Stuart onto the Lasseter Highway. Thirty miles to go, he thought, but kind of Lina to wake me. After all, we are on holiday.

Memories had also been stirred at the Mt Ebenezer, memories and the prescience of gossip: not only was the fat woman able to remember who had left the missing poster of Helen Lewis, but she also knew of Marjory Finks's disappearance.

"News travels fast down the Stuart," she said when Lina and Bingham, ready for lunch on this occasion, both ordered a 'Veggo's Delight', "We've had a couple of blokes in this morning, one with a ute, the other a copper – that's what you call them back home, isn't it? Seemed a bit worried. Said the missing woman ran an Abo gallery like the one on the poster."

"Why should that worry him, in particular?" asked Bingham.

"Didn't say. Mind you, she was a bit of a wild one."

"Who?

"The one from Alice. I only remember her dropping in here once but she made her mark. What'll you have to drink?"

"Lina?"

"I'll have a coke, please."

"And I'll have one of your northern brews – the one with the swordfish on the label. How did Marje Fink make her mark?"

"A tinnie or a stubbie?"

"Whatever's the largest, please."

"She was high as a kite when she arrived and we had some blokes in that night – musicians – they had their instruments with them – rough crowd – cowboy types dressed in leather – tattoos, the lot – and there was a bunch of women at the end of the bar. All dolled up – you know, black lace – that sort of thing. We run a nice place here but you can't be responsible for what drifts in off the highway, can you? Anyway, two of them – the women – began dancing and this Marje joined in. It was all girls together, if you get my point. They were really winding these blokes up, what with rubbing up against each other … Excuse me. What can I get for you?"

The fat woman turned to the queue behind Bingham and Lina, nodding them towards a table where they might wait for their meal to arrive. Bingham looked around: the Bull Bar, the jukebox, the large floor, the drink, the women dancing, the men watching and the heat building. When the fat woman brought their food, he asked:

"You say she made her mark."

"The blokes kept making remarks – you know the kind of thing – and this Marje was obviously enjoying herself watching them sweat. Anyway, one of them came over and asked did she mind if he sat next to her at the bar. And she – Christ, it made me laugh, the way she said it. She said, 'do you mind if I don't give a fuck'. Sorry to swear, but it was so bloody funny …"

The fat woman doubled up laughing and Lina joined her: the image of the 'cowboy type', all manly in his leathers and sporting his tattoos being told it didn't matter to Marje one way or the other where he sat was good for a laugh, if not his manhood.

"He called her a bitch – and something else – and she threw her drink in his face. It went all over him – face, jacket, crotch, the lot. I've never seen a bloke so worked up. His eyes were bloodshot from the drink, as it was. He threw his arms in the air and if one of his mates hadn't stepped in, I think he'd have hit her. As I say, she caused a bit of a stir."

"Did she say where she'd been or where she was going?" asked Bingham.

"We didn't get round to that, mate … ooh, hang on, yes she did. She'd come back from the Ayers Rock Resort and was on her way home to Alice."

Chapter Seven
THE LETTERS

Uluru was Lina's first thought when they arrived at their hotel, Sails in the Desert, Nellie Doolan was Bingham's; and they had time to spare. Sunset was around seven o'clock that evening and a few hours stretched out before them prior to their leaving the resort for the sacred rock.

On their first visit, Lina had noticed the Red Ochre Spa and she'd been tempted by either a 'Signature Journey' or a 'Massage Therapy'. Bingham suggested that the former seemed a nice idea and, in particular, the 'Desert Awakening' that offered a 'nourishing foot soak' followed by a 'full body exfoliation', 'surrender to a revitalising shower', 'body moisturisation', 'flash facial and eye reviver treatment' and a 'stimulating foot massage'. The whole experience would take a couple of hours and set Lina back $245 but Bingham thought it to be worthwhile under the circumstances.

"Which are?" asked his wife

"It'll give me a little time to nose around. I'll pay half."

"You don't want me with you?"

"It's not that, at all. It's just that I'm not sure what I'm doing. That's always irritating and I'm best avoided when I'm irritated."

It was true. No one valued his wife's contribution more than Bingham. Women – and Lina was a good example of the sex – had an uncanny knack for noticing the details in any situation, but he really didn't know what he was going to do or why or where it might lead. They were, after all, on holiday. Bingham had to keep reminding himself of that fact.

Having kissed Lina goodbye at the spa and assured her he would keep his phone switched on, his first stop was the Arkani Theatre that offered an artist in residence, an Aboriginal guide who would introduce him to the local flora and fauna, storytellers steeped in the traditions and tales of their people, dancers performing to original instruments and a possible performance by the Mani Mani Indigenous Theatre Company who were presenting The Story of Walawuru, Kakalyalya and Kaanka. If only, Bingham thought, he had the time.

The theatre entrance was small. A low door led immediately to the box office, which was about the size of a British telephone box. Beyond this and to the side, he found the entrance to the auditorium, a large floor space surrounded by tiered seats arranged in a semicircle. Theatre-in-the-round thought Bingham; back home the Sewell Barn Company in Norwich would be excited by this arrangement.

"We are not open at the moment, sir. Our season has yet to begin."

The voice came out of the dark, a deep voice Bingham always associated with speakers from the West Indies, but the man who emerged into the light was a full-blooded Aboriginal. He was silver-haired and wrinkled in that attractive way that gives human skin the appearance of tree bark. Bingham thought of Lina having her wrinkles removed at the spa and wondered, not for the first time, why the women he knew were so worried about a few wrinkles. The man held out his hand.

"David," he said, "I'm pleased to meet you."

"George – George Bingham, and I'm very pleased to meet you. I'd be right in thinking, wouldn't I, that you're Nellie Doolan's father?"

The man's deep-set eyes, which had held a merry twinkle, set first into a firm, probing stare and then crackled with laughter.

"Nellie said you had the Sight, Mr Bingham."

"I wouldn't put it as strongly as that, David. I'm only telepathic as far as my wife is concerned – she reads me like a book – but I do not, I think, possess the strange powers of your people. It was the expression in your eyes."

"You have heard that we communicate without the need for words?"

"Yes, and please, my name is George."

It had been a stroke of luck, of course, Nellie's father being the first person he met, and so soon after they'd arrived, but it would, as Bingham was to discover, have happened anyway. The two men still held each other in a handshake and, as is so often the case with like-minded people, trusted each other from the outset.

"I'm going to miss your play, am I – too early in the season?"

"We are still perfecting our performance. We open in a week's time."

"The name – what does it mean?"

"The Eagle, Cockatoo and Crow: three very important birds in the Dreamtime of my people. The eagle speaks directly to the spirit; he is the one of heightened perceptions. The crow is the sentry, guarding those places where one may not go. The cockatoo is the audacious bird, the noisy breaker of harmony."

David Doolan spoke with a cheeky smile in his eyes, tempting Bingham to raise his questions, knowing his Englishness – at least, an Englishman of Bingham's type – would consider such inquisitiveness at such a moment to be rude.

"May I show you round, George?"

Bingham smiled and nodded. As an actor himself, he was fascinated by the journey; although his mind was elsewhere, the sound system and the lighting, the special 3D effects and David Doolan's improvisations as he sketched out the story held Bingham's imagination and transported him to the ancient lands of Central Australia.

Once more in the sunshine, standing in the shade of the theatre's yellow walls, David Doolan eventually said:

"Nellie told me of your concerns."

"Helen Lewis has not returned?"

"No, and Nellie is worried more than you might imagine."

"What was she hiding?"

"You are very direct, George," replied David Doolan, with a smile.

"It was more what your daughter didn't say than what she did, David, that roused my curiosity. She was concerned, she wanted to help but something – perhaps a feeling of loyalty to Helen Lewis – held her back; and now she is fearful that her delay might prove fatal."

"You are the eagle."

"I've always had an affinity with the raven, myself."

"We know him as the undertaker of the bush, George. One must hope this is not so."

"What do you think?"

"I do not speculate. Time will tell us what has passed ... Nellie had seen letters received by Helen Lewis. They were left on the dining table ..."

"By the fruit bowl ..."

"Yes. It was unusual. Helen Lewis was very tidy ..."

Bingham waited, watching the dark face of the other man grow darker in the shadows and with the concern he felt for his daughter. He trusted Bingham, but Nellie was his daughter and he had no wish to implicate her in an act that might be perceived as intrusive and disloyal.

"She tidied them away into a drawer but could not help noticing ... She read nothing, you understand, but she noticed the writing was that of a man. She had never seen a man in Mrs Lewis's life since the death of her husband, and Nellie wondered ..."

"As anyone would ..."

"Yes ... You roused her regard for Helen Lewis's safety and Nellie thought the letters might be of help, but she had scruples about telling you of them."

"Naturally – as would any decent person."

David Doolan looked at Bingham, wondering, perhaps, whether he was to be the eagle or the raven, but feeling that one way or the other this stranger was a link to the spirit world that had so fascinated Helen Lewis. He sighed before he spoke, and when he did it was as though his heart was heavy.

"You would respect these letters?"

"Yes."

"Nellie knew you were to return and she pondered the moment."

There was an unhurried ambience in David Doolan's manner, as though tomorrow would be as fruitful as today for seeking answers, as though his spirit world would speak when it was ready, as though timelessness thread its way through all.

"I will speak with Nellie. I think this is right. Come."

Sitting in Helen Lewis's apartment, Bingham gazed at the bundle of letters before him on the table.

Nellie Doolan had let him in without a word. She took the letters from the drawer in which she had placed them almost two weeks before and put the bundle on the table. Her father had then ushered her from the room, promising to return "within the hour".

Bingham looked round the room for a second time: the vases, the cigarette box, the CDs, the stereo system, the fruit bowl (now empty), the mirror without a smear, the photographs on the shelf and the painting of Mother Earth and Father Sky. He saw Helen Lewis, reflected in the mirror, her petite frame filling the room in the way that small people do. He watched her approach the cigarette box, open it, change her mind and snap it shut. He saw her sitting on the opposite side of the table watching him as he reached out for the letters.

He was an intruder. He knew that to be true. Why was he in this position? Her disappearance was no business of his – or of anyone else's. But that wasn't true. Bingham wasn't a man who could deceive himself into such a belief. 'Am I my brother's keeper?' a schoolmaster had once asked Bingham's class when he was a boy. The answer had been obvious then and was so now.

He unfolded the first letter, and the opening greeting obliged him to put it down again. These were love letters.

My Dear, Lovely Helen ....

Those first words said so much: the writer was educated (a comma had been used when many, nowadays, do not), respected the woman and was lonely. Bingham read the signs and heard the voice.

He wouldn't read the whole letter, but just enough to locate the writer. Picking the letter up, again, he noticed the date. It was only a few months old: the second month of the year.

'... *I am free, now, but I have not been a great success at marriage, as I told you, and I wonder whether I am the right kind of person to make another commitment like that. What I don't want to do is hurt you. But I do love you ...*'

These few lines appeared soon after the opening paragraph in which the writer had asked if Helen was well. Bingham wondered how long they had known each other. Long enough for the talk to get round to marriage but how long was that these days?

Bingham glanced at the door so quietly closed by David Doolan, half expecting Helen Lewis to walk in and ask him what the hell he thought he was doing. He felt he couldn't read on and went to the kitchen. He'd had several decent cups of tea in Australia. He'd have another, making sure he washed up the cup carefully afterwards.

Back at the table, the brew steaming on a place mat, Bingham picked up the letter again.

'... *I have had a long conversation with a friend of mine. Someone who knows me well. I asked what my friend thought about my chances of making things work a second time with someone else ...*'

Bingham wasn't sure how a woman would react to such a conversation. How much did the writer know about women? Further down, Bingham came across the sentence:

'...I did not mention you, of course.'

Had the writer had second thoughts? Did he realise the mistake? Whatever the answer, the care for Helen Lewis came through. It was a man, after all. A woman wouldn't have made the same mistake and followed it up with a hurried correction. A woman would have thought ahead in matters of the heart.

'... It is a small world where we live. Even if it is a hundred miles or so between places, people know each other. I do not want you to get a bad name. I have done some silly things in my time ...'

Haven't we all? thought Bingham. Why is he making this point? He picked up the cup of tea. It was still scalding hot and Bingham gulped it down with a sense of relief. He was back home in their farmhouse kitchen, watched by the dogs in case he was thinking of enjoying a biscuit with the drink. Home was familiar – safe; other people's worlds were always disturbing.

'... I will be down next week and we can have another talk. I want things to work out between us, Helen, but ...'

Lina would have seen it as the letter of a man who was breaking off a relationship that had become too heavy for him. She would have said that there were too many 'buts' in the writing – 'buts' both seen and hidden in the phrasing.

Bingham wasn't so sure, but then he never was at this stage in an investigation. He put the letter to one side and picked up another. This one had been written many months before – December, to be precise, the beginning of the hot season in Australia; barbecues on the beach for Christmas dinner.

'... *I cannot tell you how much that week in Adelaide meant to me. Just to be with you and walk along the main street where the cafes and restaurants open onto the pavement. I do not need anything else in my life ... Our visit to Cleland Park and you having your picture taken with the koala ...I loved Adelaide with you ... I could be happy there again ... I loved the cinema ... And the people seemed to love us, didn't they ...I think they could see we were happy ...'*

Bingham found the writing to be effusive, but Lina wouldn't have agreed with that assessment. Thinking of her, he remembered their first meeting, which they'd talked about when last in Yulara. He remembered the foyer of the Coliseum and the Concert Hall in Prague, where they spent their honeymoon: places he had never forgotten and could see quite clearly as he sat in Helen Lewis's apartment. Places were important to people in love: conservation parks, cinemas, street-side restaurants in the sun.

The letter was signed 'Chuck', like the first one. It suggested not only a nickname but one associated with manliness. Had he made it up or had Helen Lewis?

How long had this couple known each other? Bingham, less reticent now, rifled back through the letters. The first one or two were dated September and October of the previous year: dates that indicated more or less the end of the tourist season in the Red Centre if not the rest of the country. When he and Lina arrived in March, activities were just about to open up. In Alice Springs, the season seemed to run from April through to

August, when the weather was cool enough to enjoy the scenery and the festivals.

So where had they met? Was Helen looking for next year's arts and crafts along the Stuart? When had Chuck visited Yulara? Why had he come to the resort? Was it Chuck who placed the missing posters? Had Chuck any idea that Helen was going to disappear? How did Helen feel about Chuck?

Bingham saw a calm woman: not one given to wild passions but a woman who calculated.

He had no real picture of Chuck. Chuck eluded him. At one moment he was a bloke: at another ... Bingham walked to the window that looked out over the spruce-clean compound of the Ayers Rock Resort and tried to picture the man walking towards the apartment. He was not a man like Helen's first husband, who Bingham saw as quiet and studious. Chuck was a man in transition, and Helen Lewis had started the process.

He returned to the dining table and picked up one of the earlier letters.

'*Dear Helen,*

It was nice to spend the evening with you. I enjoyed our meal together ...'

Bingham smiled. The tone was polite. It could almost have been a thank-you letter to an aunt one saw only occasionally but whose company was always pleasant. Where had they enjoyed their meal together? Not, Bingham thought, at the Ayers Rock Resort. He looked down the page and noticed the handwriting for the first time. It wasn't an elegant hand, but neither was it clumsy; functional was the word that came to Bingham's mind; a hand learned in school but not much used afterwards. And then another thought struck him: all the letters were handwritten! Whoever wrote by hand these days? Bingham always typed his on the computer and often apologised if the correspondent was a personal friend; but this man actually wrote his letters on writing paper!

There were people who never wrote at all, but merely texted their messages. He knew people who had ended relationships on a text. '*Wonderful, magical time but goodbye forever*' was the message a young man had sent the friend of one of his daughters. Bingham had favoured a backside being kicked, but his daughter, Cecilia, had said 'it was the modern way'.

Chuck wasn't modern, then?

'... *I would like us to meet again. I know it is difficult but I will be in Adelaide for a few days next week and I wondered if ...*'

He 'wondered if': Bingham smiled again. He liked Chuck; at least, he liked the Chuck of the early letters. Where had they had the meal together if it wasn't Yulara? Was it where they had met? Bingham read on.

'... *Perhaps next time we could spend a few days in Adelaide? I do not mean anything by that, just that it would be good to get to know each other. It's a nice place. There is lots to do and see. I think you would like the old market and there is Cleland Conservation Park where you can have your photograph taken with a koala and feed a wallaby ...*'

Chuck went on in the same tone, talking of having lunch at Brunellis, tea at The Coffee Spot in the arcade, the Victoria Gardens, taking a tram from Mosely Square and a walk from the North Terrace. Only this letter was signed simply 'R'; the man's nickname had not yet arrived, but who on earth was 'R' and why hadn't he used his full name?

Bingham rummaged through the letters again, especially the early ones, but there were no further clues to who Helen Lewis's lover might have been. He'd almost finished when his phone rang.

"Bing, where are you?"

Bingham was annoyed: annoyed at himself for not remembering, annoyed at Lina for phoning. They'd arranged to meet after her spa session, and he hadn't realised the time.

"In Helen Lewis's apartment, reading her letters."

"What are you doing?"

"I'm sorry, Lina. I didn't notice the time. I'll explain when I get to you. Hmm, can you go along to that little café on the square, and I'll meet you there. Order the ... uhm drinks, and I'll be with you as soon as I can."

"How long will you be?"

"I have to wait for someone to let me out of the apartment. I can't just leave."

"The coach leaves for Uluru after lunch, Bing. We haven't got all day."

"I know, I know. I won't be long ... Will I recognise you?"

Bingham had mastered the art of changing the subject, but Lina wasn't to be diverted.

"Have you any idea how long you'll be?"

"Not long ..."

It was one of those conversations that would in some marriages end in a row and in others dissolve into nothing; either way, it would lead nowhere useful. Bingham looked at his watch. How long had he been? He wasn't sure.

"Fifteen minutes," he said, not because it might be true but because he had no idea.

"What shall I get you to drink?"

"A glass of the local red, please."

"Don't be long, will you?"

Bingham had no idea, but the phone call focussed his mind and he turned to the letters realising he hadn't looked at the envelopes. Some were postmarked 'Adelaide', others 'Darwin' and one 'Alice Springs'.

As he returned the letters to their original state, the door opened and David and Nellie Doolan came into the room.

"I lost track of the time," said Bingham, "I'll just wash up this cup. I hope you don't mind but I fancied a cup of tea and ..."

"Please, don't worry, Mr Bingham. I'll see to the cup."

"Have the letters been helpful, George?"

"I'm not sure. Nellie. Did Mrs Lewis have any men friends?"

"I don't know. I don't think so."

"But you would have known, wouldn't you, if she had entertained them here?"

"I never met any of her friends."

"The letters were from a man and they were affectionate letters dating back almost a year. Are you sure ...?"

"I don't know."

"Mrs Lewis never spoke of a man whose name began with R?"

"No."

"Cast your mind back to last December, Nellie. Mrs Lewis spent time – probably a week – in Adelaide. Did she mention this to you?"

"I clean for her, Mr Bingham. I am not her ... confidant."

"But you are the kind of person in whom someone might confide, aren't you – especially a woman in matters of the heart?"

Nellie Doolan smile, and Bingham realised she felt flattered.

"She came back very happy from Adelaide. She said she had had a nice time ... It took her out of herself. She had been low since Mr Lewis's death."

"Do you know where she first met the man she called Chuck?"

"She never mentioned his name."

"But you knew she'd been with a man friend?"

"Yes."

"Can you guess where they might have met? Where else might she have gone?"

"There are only the roadhouses and the communities where she buys her artworks."

"Did she ever go to Alice Springs?"

"Sometimes. We all do."

"You see, someone cares enough about Helen to have written her tender letters. It might be helpful to find that person."

"Do you think he might be involved in her disappearance?" asked David Doolan, interrupting Bingham's questioning for the first time.

"I have no idea, but from what I have heard Helen Lewis isn't the kind of person who would simply go off, leaving people to worry about where she might be. It's clear she had a chatty relationship with Nellie. If she had gone walkabout, she is most likely to have spoken about it, particularly as Nellie knows more about the

Dreamtime than anyone else in Helen's life – as far as we know."

Bingham's phone rang. He sighed.

"I must go. I said I'd meet my wife for lunch. Look, Nellie, I only want to help Mrs Lewis. Lina and I are here until tomorrow. If there's anything else – anything at all – that might lead us to find her, please let me know."

"Yes, of course."

The young woman was so composed that it almost annoyed Bingham to see her wipe the cup, shine it with a dry cloth and replace it carefully in the cupboard. Watching her pour the excess water from the kettle and unplug it didn't relieve his sense of frustration. But she had agreed to him reading the letters, and so she must be concerned, mustn't she?

"Goodbye for now, and thank you," said Bingham, shaking both father and daughter by the hand before hurrying off to find Lina.

She sat at an outside table of the Gecko's Café in the shade but enveloped by the warmth of the sun. The temperature had risen to its usual 40 degrees and no doubt the flies were annoying people wherever they could but in the shade of the Yulara sails it was pleasant enough; the wine was cool and the pizza putanesca, which they shared, hot.

When Bingham had relayed the gist of the letters, Lina asked the question that had also troubled him.

"Why the secrecy, Bing: these are grownups we're talking about – not teenagers – and neither of them was married to anyone else – or was he?"

"In a small community gossip may well be the spice at everyone's dinner table. Perhaps she wasn't the kind of person who liked people knowing about her private life."

"Or he didn't!"

"Yes, possibly. If only, we knew who the man was and where they met."

"Well, that shouldn't be too difficult to find out, should it?"

"What do you mean?"

"Come on, Bing, you're the one who usually attaches so much importance to the odd word in a conversation."

Chapter Eight
THE SACRED ROCK

It was not to Bingham's credit that he found Uluru less than interesting and the fault could certainly not be placed at the foot of the sacred rock. He'd foolishly expected to find himself alone in a wide expanse of desert, traipsing through dry grass and acacia shrubs, surrounded by the trilling of insects, invaded by the silence of the dying day with Uluru towering above him as the colours of the monolith changed from a dull sandy colour to black.

He hadn't reckoned with the line of coaches behind him, the fence in front and the eagerness of his fellow travels to be first for a seat and first at the table and for the million or so flies to be very active at sunset. Lina and he donned their veils again, but the devourers of carrion settled everywhere: on the breads, in the champagne glasses and amongst the salads before settling for the array of cheeses.

It was a glorious evening, as Lina reminded him when she sensed a certain grumpiness settling in from where she sat talking to a group of other women. They were up against the fence and so low down that Bingham wondered whether they'd see the rock at all.

He'd offered to catch its fading moments on camera, a task that obliged him to take a photograph every ten minutes. His first shot caught the bright sandiness of the rock and later ones passed through burnt red to brown and then purple, mauve and an earthy blue to eventual blackness; but at no time could it be said that the rock remained as either one colour or the other. As the sun set upon it, the colours mingled, and so the early sandiness contained the later mauves, the final blues and traces of the lighter colours; throughout, an underlying darkness pervaded every colour change.

For no reason that he could think of at the time, the changing colours suggested human nature to Bingham. Whatever the moment, whatever the time, whatever the occasion, whatever the incident, whatever the flux of circumstances, the thread of personality ran through all things, suffering long, envying not, seeking not its own, thinking no evil, bearing all things, enduring all things – or not. It wasn't at that moment the answer came to him, but only the suggestion of a possibility.

Their excursion also offered a sunrise experience, a chance grabbed by both Lina and Bingham. Whether he slept heavily or restlessly, Bingham never rose later than six o'clock on any morning back home. Since the Uluru sunrise occurred at about that time, he was pleased to be back at the fence sans food, sans champagne, sans an overload of coaches but accompanied by an Aboriginal girl and her sister, both fresh from Melbourne, both keen to experience the sacred murmurings of their ancestors.

Although Bingham was "on the quiet side" (as his mother used to say), Lina was chatty and tended to draw people to her; the Aboriginal girls were no exception and were soon sharing their thoughts. The Dreamtime stories of mythical beings seemed real to them: the little boy who came from nowhere, the Valley of the Winds, the scars in the rock face where the spears of giants landed, the caves and hollows where the ancestors gathered, the boomerang that captured the sun, the creeping insects that ravaged the land and death coming into the world, emerging from a crevice in the rock.

"When the curlew men and women emerged from the crevice in the rock, the women came first and brought dissension with them. Dissension turned to anger, and the bone of death was pointed at the first man to come. He was buried in the stony ground, but the following day the earth shook, and he pushed himself from the grave and looked accusingly at those around him, especially at the other men. But Urbura the magpie raced to the rescue. He speared the undead man in the throat and drove him back into the ground. Urbura then flew off with the curlew women. His killing of the first man a second time brought death into the world."

Bingham looked at the two young women. They were obviously of mixed race: too pale to be true Aboriginals.

"Our father was from Poland," said the older of the two girls in answer to his question, "Dad was a geologist when he arrived here, but now works in a bakery."

"Why?"

"It was the only way he could keep a roof over our heads, he said. He has no time for these old stories, unlike mum who wants us to re-connect with the culture of her ancestors."

"And you? How do you feel?"

"We belong here," answered the younger girl, emphatically and with a smile, "the Aboriginals say we don't, that the land is theirs by rights, but this is where we were born. We've never been to Poland. In fact, we've never been out of Australia."

"You're doing this to please your mum?" suggested Lina.

"Yes. There has to be a middle ground somewhere and it has to be where the two cultures come together."

"You're the future," said Bingham.

"We're steering a path that way," said the older girl, laughing loudly, "As we told mum, you can't go back to what life was like before the white people arrived, but maybe we can learn something from what our ancestors had to say."

Young Australians, thought Bingham, and felt happier, as they walked back to the coach, than he had since his realisation at sunset the previous day.

"Bing, would it be sensible for me to stay on here?"

"Why?"

"You know why. You're going to be worrying away at Helen Lewis's disappearance until she turns up or ... is found. I know you, and I can tell that the answer lies either here or back in Alice Springs – or, probably, in both places and between the two. I'm right, aren't I?"

"I've never known you to be wrong, Lina."

"Never mind the sarcasm, Bing – I'm being serious. You want to talk to this Bob Evans about why he put up those posters, but you're still convinced that the answer lies at Yularu ..."

"I thought we were flying on tomorrow."

"That's a detail and – as you're always saying when you leave me to arrange the holidays – women are good at the details. The Aussies are easy-going people. They'll sort something out. We're not at home now, where they charge you more for changing your mind than you paid for the original flight."

"How will I get you back?"

Lina laughed and hugged him: the play on the old joke always amused her.

"I'm sure I can find a way ... but it's most likely to be you returning here, isn't it?"

"It looks that way," replied Bingham, kissing his wife lightly on the lips, "yes, I think the answer will be here rather than in Alice."

So, it was agreed that Lina should stay on if there was a room available, and after an exhaustive, and exhausting, search the receptionist found she was "able to squeeze you in".

Driving along the Lasseter Highway towards the Stuart and, eventually, Alice Springs, Bingham sank back into the comfort of his seat and pretended to be asleep. One of the other passengers, a woman who never stopped talking on the way down, had decided he needed company – and, anyway, was curious as to why Lina had "left him". Not wishing to engage with the woman and resort to a string of music hall jokes, Bingham dozed off.

From the window of the coach, under half-closed eyes, he watched the box trees and the bottlebrush shrubs in the ridges of scarlet sand and the ochre sun rising above the red desert. It was that time of day when, at a weekend, Lina might still be dozing back home, wondering whether to get up and cook their breakfast. Less than a dozen metres in front of the coach, a red kangaroo hopped across the tarmac, and their driver swerved to prevent an accident.

He was reminded of coming across Tony McDonald's car stacked partway up a tree on their first day out from Adelaide; had he not avoided hitting a kangaroo, they'd never have met Nellie Doolan or heard of Helen Lewis.

He squinted and glimpsed the roadside again. In the early light he saw a group of ring-necked parakeets bunched together on the branches of a gum tree. Lina would have liked to have seen those, he thought. He felt guilty at leaving her behind; she was right, of course, but it didn't seem fair. After all, they were on holiday. How many times had he made that remark?

Bingham saw a busy evening and following morning ahead. Hopefully, Lina would have further chats with Nellie Doolan. She might even get the chance to re-read those letters and might come across another clue. Something in the writing, perhaps, that might take them just a step further along the road to find Helen Lewis, the woman who had disappeared without trace and for no apparent reason.

Back in Alice, he'd find Bob Evans. The man had said he lived there, hadn't he: surely, that wasn't a false memory or the lack of one. Memory was the very devil at Bingham's age: yesterday sometimes seemed further away than his childhood.

Then, of course, there was the other woman – Marjory Fink – who had also vanished without a word, although in her case friends thought it not unusual. Marje was a character: someone who always did her own thing, her own way. Nevertheless, surely it was unusual for two women who lived within what in Australia was a few miles of each other, and who both ran Aboriginal art galleries, to have disappeared within a few days of each other? There must be a connection, mustn't there? 'Happenstance', 'coincidence' … what was the final phrase? He'd read it somewhere, years ago, in a James Bond novel, while on the train back to university. Ah yes, 'enemy action'. That was it, but who was the enemy, if there was one at all?

"Wake up, we're at the roadhouse."

The garrulous woman gave him a nudge, not as gently as Lina would have done but he was grateful: it was time for coffee and Alice Springs seemed to be a million miles along the highway.

Katy, the young woman who worked in the gallery, knew Bob Evans's address and Bingham was soon knocking on the door of a small apartment on the outskirts of Alice Springs, thanks to another extortionate taxi ride. Bob Evans's 'place' (modern terminology always sounded as though it was borrowed from the Americans, to Bingham, although he couldn't imagine the Australians borrowing anything from anybody despite the cabbie having used it) was in a small area of what back home would be called 'flats', several sharing the same external balcony.

A young woman opened the door. Smart as paint, thought Bingham with a smile, as the old phrase occurred to him. He remembered how clean, almost dapper, Bob Evans had looked – hair neatly combed, boots highly polished – and concluded that this young woman was his daughter or … no, Bingham didn't entertain the idea.

"I'm looking for Bob Evans," he said.

"Who's looking?" replied the girl.

Bingham didn't like the tone of her reply: he had an aversion to cockiness, which, to him, approached rudeness. It's surprising how much offence can be injected into two words.

"My wife and I met Bob a few days ago. He was … *seemed* concerned that a lady friend of his was missing …"

"Which one was that?" replied the girl with a knowing laugh.

"Marjory Fink …"

"Oh, Marje! I can't see dad being too bothered about Marje. She's a tough nut is Marje."

"He said it was a bit of a worry," persisted Bingham.

The girl laughed. She was dressed in tight jeans and a loose, off-the-shoulder top. Her naturally wavy hair flopped around her head and down almost to her shoulders. Her face was tanned and shining. Bingham didn't think she could be more than eighteen but realised you never can tell – not these days: she might be in her late twenties.

"Is your dad home or about anywhere?"

"He might be. He's back in town."

The girl expressed no curiosity about Bingham's visit, and that struck him as strange: but then, she might not be interested in anything that didn't concern her directly.

"If I give you my phone number, will you ask him to ring me?"

"I might … when he gets in."

She hadn't meant to add the last phrase: truculence was obviously her style, but an old-fashioned courtesy lurked somewhere in the background.

"Come in," she said, "Dad won't be long. He's gone for some groceries."

The apartment was neat and tidy except for the girl's personal belongings, which were dumped everywhere: shoes kicked off in the hallway, coat slung over a chair, handbag dropped onto the table.

"I'll just tidy this up before Dad gets back. He shouldn't be long. He popped out when I got home. I'm starving."

Bingham didn't ask why she hadn't brought some food in with her if she was as hungry as she said but he kept quiet.

"I'm Nicky, by the way – after Nicole Kidman. Mum liked her. Thought she'd got sass."

"George, George Bingham – pleased to meet you."

He wasn't but it didn't pay to say so.

"You know something about Marje, do you," asked Nicky.

"No. I take it she's not returned?"

"Not that I know of."

"Your dad hasn't said anything."

Nicky Evans shrugged. It clearly didn't matter to her whether he had or not, at least as far as Marje Fink was concerned. Frustrated by the girl's off-hand manner, Bingham decided to verge on the offensive.

"Your dad's a widower, is he?"

"What makes you say that?"

"Your home is nice but it lacks a woman's touch," he said.

"You've got a bloody cheek."

"So, my wife says."

"Mum buggered off years ago when we lived in Brisbane. She was a bitch. Always at dad, even when there was nothing to complain about, she was at him. Enjoyed it, see. There're women like that."

"I know. I've met them occasionally. You stayed with your dad?"

"I wasn't going to live with that bitch. I'd never know who she was going to bring home next. The last straw was her accusing dad of trying to run her over. Dad – a trucker! She was always going on about his driving, and he ignored her – knowing how crap she was herself. But that was the last straw – her saying he'd backed into her on the driveway. He called his lawyer the same day, and that was that, as they say."

Bingham had got what he wanted but didn't feel proud of the fact, any more than he felt good about disliking the girl. She'd had her problems and dealt with them in the only way she knew how. Divorce is always destructive, and she must have been little more than a child when it happened. Bingham wondered how promiscuous the mother might have been: clearly, Bob didn't get a divorce on the basis that his wife had criticised his driving.

"I'm sorry to hear that," he said, "I didn't mean to pry. You did well to stand by your dad. He must be proud of you."

Nicky Evans smiled with what seemed a forced reluctance.

"He's OK. We get on. He won't be long – I keep saying that! Can I get you a coffee?"

"A cup of tea would be nice," replied Bingham, "Australia's only one of two places in the world, outside Britain, where you can get a decent cup of tea."

"Where's the other?" called Nicky Evans from the kitchen.

"The Falkland Islands."

"You've been there?" asked the girl appearing from the kitchen, caddy in hand. "Blimey – you're well-travelled."

"My wife and I get about."

She laughed, a genuine one for the first time, Bingham thought.

They were still talking about travelling when Bob Evans came through the door, three bags of groceries in his hands and the door key between his teeth.

"George?"

"Bob – we met at Marje's art gallery. You were dropping off ..."

"I remember. I just didn't expect to find you here when I got home. Has Marje ... no, she'd have rung."

"It wasn't about Marje I came to see you ..."

Bingham hadn't meant to pause. It only happened because he was suddenly aware that Nicky might not know about Helen Lewis.

"Go on – you want me to drop you off some wine?" suggested Bob with a laugh from the kitchen where he'd gone to settle the groceries.

Bingham remained silent until Bob re-entered the living room and then in his quietest voice said:

"It's about the posters you've put up about Helen Lewis's disappearance."

"Right ... Nicky, you done that tea yet?"

"It's now coming. Do you want coffee, Dad?"

"No, no, I'll go with the tea. You get the food started, will you?"

"Da-ad, I've just got in!"

"So have I, and George and I need a chat."

Nicky dumped, rather than placed, the mugs of tea on the table and slouched off. Bob Evans rose and shut the door before turning his attention to Bingham.

"Nicky's a bit touchy about my lady friends," he said, assuming a laugh, "What makes you think I put up some posters about ... about Mrs Lewis?"

"Lina and I asked when we first stopped off at the roadhouses. No one could remember who put up the posters, then, but they'd been talking about it and when we returned they'd remembered."

"Are you a private detective or something?"

"No, no. My wife and I are on holiday ..."

"So, what's your interest in ... Mrs Lewis?"

"The first time we stopped off at Yulara we were told she'd disappeared and that it was unlike her not to say where she was going ..."

"So?"

"We then saw the posters you'd put up at the Mt Ebenezer ..."

"Yeah, I get that – but why are you interested?"

"I've come to ask you the same question."

Bob Evans shot a glance at the kitchen door. From beyond it came the clatter of saucepans and the scrape of utensils.

"I can meet you at a bar if you'd rather talk elsewhere," suggested Bingham.

"I put up the posters because I was concerned that ... Mrs Lewis had disappeared – like you."

"You knew her?"

"I drop off supplies at Yulara. We'd met."

"Bob – each time you've mentioned her by name, you've paused before calling her 'Mrs Lewis' rather than Helen. It wasn't just a matter of having *met* her, was it?"

"I don't see that's any of your business ... George."

"But, like me, you want to find her – or, at least, know she's safe?"

"That's why I put up the posters."

Bingham wasn't one to be closed down.

"But you didn't put up any about Marje."

"Marje is different."

"So, people keep saying – but she is missing, just like Helen Lewis, and you were concerned enough about Helen Lewis to alert people's attention to the fact that she *was* missing."

"I said, Helen's …"

"… different?"

"Yes."

"So, you knew her well?"

"Look, I think it's time we brought this conversation to an end."

"You knew her well?"

"I said …"

"You want to find her?"

"Yes."

"So, tell me what you know. Have you made other enquiries?"

"No one's seen hide nor hair of her since she disappeared."

"What do you think may have happened?"

"I haven't a clue."

"Given that she was a person considerate enough to let people know where she might be going, the only alternative is that she was abducted – for want of a better word."

"What do you mean?"

"I don't mean anything … Had she any close friends?"

"Like?"

"Women friends, a lover – someone she might have visited quietly, without wanting to make a song and dance about it?"

"What makes you ask?"

"Someone she might have gone off with," suggested Bingham.

"I don't know what you're getting at."

"Did she know Marje Fink?"

"Why should she?"

"They were in the same line of business. It seems unlikely that they never met."

"I don't think so."

"Don't think it unlikely or don't think they ever met?"

"Look, George, I think you've asked enough questions. I'm concerned about ... about Mrs Lewis – she seemed to be a nice lady – and so I put up the posters, just in case, but Marje is different. She'll come back when she's ready ... and to be frank, I don't see what you can do about either of the ladies disappearing, since you're here on holiday and will be flying off to somewhere else pretty soon, if I'm not mistaken. Right?"

"We were due to fly to Cairns tomorrow."

"Just my point! So, are you just being bloody nosey?"

"But now we're not."

"Not what?"

"Not flying to Cairns tomorrow. My wife's postponing the flight. She's at Yulara, now. You see, Bob, there's something odd about Helen's disappearance and my wife and I are going to find out what it is. It may or may not be connected with Marj's, and it may or may not be connected with you. It just strikes me that anyone who might be interested in finding either of the ladies would do well to share what they know."

"If I think of anything else, I'll let you know."

Bob Evans was put out: his tone said it all. Bingham wasn't, as he was shown to the door. Was any more proof needed? He thought not. Involving the police wasn't Bingham's intention – not yet, anyway, but, in the end, he might have no other option.

Chapter Nine
THE ELDER

It was late afternoon, the time of day when Alice Springs looked tired, as any hot country looks tired if its people haven't enjoyed the afternoon siesta common throughout those European countries that border the Mediterranean. In Italy, where he and Lina had spent a great deal of time, a town would be coming to life; here, it seemed reluctant to finish the day.

A group of Aboriginal men were flopped out on the small grassy banks that edged the pathway from the precinct, where Marjory Fink had her gallery, to the entrance of Todd Mall; weary shoppers were spilling from the mall on their way home with today's dinner and a few youngsters hung around by the old toilets Bingham had been advised not to use. He looked about him, unsure what to do or where to go. What was he doing here? What business of his was any of this? He felt failure waiting round the next corner and foolishness not far away.

On the few other occasions, he'd investigated a disappearance there had always been people to ask, some who were actually interested in finding the missing person, others who certainly wanted to give that impression, true or false. Here, no one seemed bothered.

Why should they be? Was anyone really missing? Was there any reason to suspect foul play if they were?

He wandered back to the precinct and went into the gallery. Katy, the young assistant was leaning against the cash desk, a mug of coffee in her hand.

"Marje's still not back," she said, without waiting for Bingham to enquire, "If you ask me, she's in Adelaide on a bender. It's happened before."

"When?"

"When she's been upset about something – men, usually."

"Does she have a steady man friend?"

"Apart from Bob, you mean – no, not really. At least as far as I know."

"Has Bob upset her before?"

"She thought he was carrying on with someone else up in Tennant Creek."

"Was he?"

"I wouldn't put it past him, but she never said. She was proud that way – liked to think she was in charge. You know."

"Some women find men like that to be a bit of a challenge," said Bingham, "That's part of the attraction."

Katy looked at him as though she wasn't expecting an old man to know such things.

"Do you have her phone number?"

"She isn't answering, but I'll give it to you if you like."

"Thanks. It might be useful."

"What do you think is happening?"

"I don't know, but I have the impression that in the end it's going to be something very simple," replied Bingham.

"What makes you say that?"

"It's a feeling I have – nothing more," Bingham answered, taking the slip of paper on which the girl had written Marje's number. "Do you know where Henry lives?"

"I wouldn't trouble him if I were you. He's ugly when he's in a bad mood."

"Is he still in one?"

"It's like a habit with him – easier to be horrible than be nice."

"His girlfriend seems nice."

"It's what you were saying – she finds him a challenge. He'll be round to close the shop soon. If you really want to see him, why not wait and have a drink at Reg's?"

"I'll do that. Thanks, Katy."

Bingham sat in the café with a schooner of local beer and waited. It was pleasant enough just sitting; the sun was cutting through the window but the air-conditioning kept the temperatures bearable and he dozed off, his head resting on his knuckles. He was woken by the young waitress tapping him on the shoulder.

"Henry Fink has just arrived and your beer's gone warm," she said.

How she knew he was waiting for Henry, Bingham was unsure, but waking him was thoughtful. He looked up and saw Henry standing at the bar, and his question was answered.

"I understand you want to see me," said the young man, a slight sneer playing round his mouth, "Fern says you mean well and that I should be polite."

"Only if you want to," replied Bingham, half awake and suddenly fed up with the whole business: his beer was as sour as Henry Fink's expression, and he wondered, for the second time in just a few hours, why he was bothering.

"Mum hasn't been to see any of our relatives," said Henry, sitting across the table from Bingham and shoving his beer glass forward for no apparent reason.

Bingham didn't like to ask if this worried him in case Henry found the very thought annoying; and, suddenly, Bingham felt he'd lost his patience with the boy.

"What do you want to know?" asked Henry, eager it seemed to place the initiative with Bingham.

"Nothing, really. My wife and I are off to Cairns soon. We should have gone when we intended. If there's anything amiss in this business, the time will come when the police can sort it out ... And the time will come."

"You're convinced there's foul play?"

"A man is involved in a relationship with two women, one of whom seems to have marriage in mind. What's that a recipe for?"

"Are you talking about Bob Evans?"

Bingham nodded; he didn't feel able to do or say any more.

"He seemed all right to me," said Henry.

"No doubt."

Bingham could simply have said 'yes', but he wanted the young man to feel his judgement was being questioned.

"You don't like him?"

"I don't know him – do you?"

"Not very well. Who's this other woman?"

"You don't know?"

"Mum never talked to me about ... about her private life."

It seemed odd, in such a small community, that anyone might have a private life. When Bingham was a child, everything to do with adults was private, but nowadays parents seemed to share everything with their children. Not, he thought, that that was what children needed. He looked at the young man, wondering what to say next. He didn't want to put a question; he wanted Henry to be the interrogator. In the young man's eyes, he saw a mixture of anger and bemusement.

"Your girlfriend would know," said Bingham.

"Fern?!"

It was an exclamation of disbelief that a mere girlfriend might know more than he did, as well as a question.

"Ask her."

"Ask her what?"

"If she knows the identity of the other woman in Bob Evans's life. Women are very good at knowing such things."

"What might that have to do with Mum?"

"You don't know a great deal about your mum's comings and goings do you? Like most sons you take little interest in such things, but women are fascinated by them. Ask Fern."

Henry banged on the window, and Bingham looked up. Fern was across at the gallery.

"Try opening the door, son," called the barman, "unless you want to pay for a broken window."

"I'll go."

It was the young waitress who spoke and she was as good as her word. Within a few minutes, Fern sat beside Henry at the table, a smile on her face for Bingham.

"Hello," she said, "You haven't found Marje yet, then?"

"Can I buy you a drink?" asked Bingham.

"I'll have a tinnie," said Fern, with a laugh, supposing Bingham might wonder what that might be.

"Do you know whether Bob Evans had a fancy woman?" asked Henry, without regard for Fern's place in the conversation.

"Is that what you've been talking about?"

"Yes. Our friend here thinks you know more than I do."

"That's almost certainly true," said Fern, winking at Bingham.

"Well?"

"Girl talk, Henry – not something you've ever shown much interest in, unlike Mr Bingham here."

"Did he have a fancy woman?"

"I don't see what this has to do with anything," replied Fern.

"Mum might have gone to sort her out."

"The 'fancy woman' – to use your expression – disappeared before your mother," said Bingham.

"You knew he had one!"

"I asked around," said Bingham, smiling at the young woman

"She was down at Yulara, was she?" asked Fern.

Bingham nodded, not being sure how many 'shes' or sheilas, to use the local expression, might be involved or, for that matter, how many blokes. The letters had a tenderness about them that suggested a genuine affection, but affection and circumstances were often apt to collide. Who was then the winner?

He wasn't sure what he was looking for in this conversation with these two who were little more than children in as much as they'd never had anyone to worry about except themselves. It was their impression of Bob Evans he wanted, Bob Evans who had been eager to get Bingham out of his apartment when he didn't wish to acknowledge the depth of his relationship with Helen Lewis.

"What did this other woman do for a living?" asked Fern.

"She was in the same business as Marje," replied Bingham.

"And you say she disappeared as well? Isn't that weird?"

"And no one is looking for either of them except, perhaps, Bob Evans, who did put missing posters in the roadhouses along the Stuart – at least, for the other woman if not for your mother, Henry."

"What did you say?"

"You heard."

"What's he playing at?"

"He wasn't concerned about your mother's disappearance."

"What?"

"Were you? Did you think about making enquiries?"

Henry Fink glared at Bingham, who thought he might be about to receive a punch in the mouth, and then at Fern. He stood quickly, jolting the table and almost spilling his beer into Bingham's lap.

"Well, you didn't, did you?" said Fern, moving aside, as her boyfriend shoved past and made for the door.

"Sorry about that," said Bingham.

"No, you're not. You said it deliberately," laughed the girl, "and I can't say I blame you. He is a prick."

Lina wasn't too surprised when, as she sat in the sun outside Geckos Café enjoying a latte and waiting,

David Doolan, who she recognised from Bingham's description, approached and asked if he might join her.

She had no expectations of her stay at the Ayers Rock resort other than she might be useful to her husband. In his earlier searches for missing people, Bingham had always emphasised the importance of place: 'a sense of place' was his expression, being where the person he was looking for had last been seen.

She liked both David Doolan and his daughter. Her female instincts told her that neither of these two people knew more than they were saying, that neither had anything to do with Helen Lewis's disappearance; but she wasn't so sure about Bingham's thoughts on the matter, and his instincts were good.

After all, his instincts had persuaded her that they would have a happy marriage, when she had hesitated, and he had been right. She loved Bing; sometimes, she thought she loved him more than her children, but he always assured her that wasn't possible and that no decent husband would mind if it were not true.

"Your husband has his doubts about Nellie, doesn't he Mrs Bingham?" asked David Doolan when he joined her with a black coffee and a blueberry muffin.

"Bing keeps an open mind, until he's sure. A friend of ours – an ex-policeman – once told us that the art of investigation is to explore possibilities, confirm the negatives and eliminate all explanations of what might have happened until only one remains; and that is what Bing is doing – with very little cooperation from anybody, I might add. Oh, and please call me Lina."

"I think it's the first time I have come across that name."

"My father was a fan of the American singer, Lena Horne, and wanted me christened with her name. My mother, who was Italian, agreed on the condition that he spelt it the Italian way: 'i' in Italian has the long 'e' sound. My middle name is my mother's – Eva – pronounced 'eh-va', just to confuse things further. What's on your mind, David?"

"You're very direct, Lina."

"It's a bad habit I've picked up from my husband."

David Doolan was embarrassed: he didn't know what to make of this English woman. The attitude of most Australians around Alice towards his people was quite clear – they accepted your culture and liked you or they didn't – but this woman represented untrodden ground. Was this what was called English reserve?

"Did your mother have problems being accepted when she came to England?"

"Some, I believe. The English and the Italians had been on opposite sides during the war, as I expect you know. My father was in the army and met my mother when his regiment made its way into Italy after the North African campaign. They fell in love and he brought her home, where they were married. She never complained about prejudice and the villagers loved her – but then, that generation never did complain, did they – they'd been through too much not to be grateful for the Peace."

"We have to stand up for ourselves, Lina."

"Yes, of course the world is different now … What can I do for you, David?"

"It's more a question of what I can do for you, I think. I have been talking to my daughter and we have come up with an idea …"

He paused and looked around at the virtually empty square, as though what he was about to propose was a secret that should be known only to him and Lina. Under the huge sail-like parasols, the day was cool. It was hard to believe that only a few hundred yards away there was desert, the Red Centre of the continent, unexplored and untraversed except by David Doolan's people who had walked the land for 50,000 years.

"Your husband wondered whether Mrs Lewis might have been tempted into the desert. He thought she might have been drawn into what my people call the Dreamtime. This is right, is it not?"

"We thought it was possible but ... she would not have gone without saying so ..."

"But she knew the pathways."

"I'm sorry – pathways?"

"The Pathways to the Dreaming."

"This is the first anyone has mentioned pathways ..."

"Mrs Lewis had been with Nellie before she disappeared. She knew the pathways. If Mrs Lewis is out there, Nellie can take you to where she would be."

"Nellie has nothing to prove to me, David. Besides, if she was in any way complicit in Helen Lewis's disappearance, Nellie has left it rather late in the day to ... well, clear her name. Helen has been missing for ... what, about two weeks, hasn't she?"

"My daughter was not involved in Mrs Lewis's disappearance in any way. She wishes only to show good faith."

Lina looked at the young woman's father. She was afraid. She acknowledged that fact to herself but could not see how this man or his daughter could do her harm. It was a gentle face – not the face of a scoundrel, not a face that wished her ill. Lina imagined the young woman, anxious since Helen's disappearance working herself into a state. That was it; that is all it was.

"Will you go?"

"Yes."

"Thank you. It will put Nellie's mind at rest. But first you must understand, and there is someone I would like you to meet. He is the Elder of our clan. He will explain."

It wasn't far, just out beyond the resort where the desert clung dryly to the edge of a rough pathway and then a little further until they came to a rock ledge that overhung a pool. Under the ledge, sat a man so old Lina thought he could barely be alive. He had David Doolan's voice, deep and rich, but hushed to a whisper, and the same dark, tree bark skin, but drawn of all moisture; his hair was a shock of white as though flakes of manna had settled on his head long ago and decided to stay.

He smiled at Lina and gestured her to a rock so she was close enough to be able to hear him and far enough away to not feel imposed upon. The hand that gestured reached out and she took it in hers and the skin crackled as they exchanged greetings. She'd read enough to know that this was a privilege, that she sat where the men sat discussing men's business.

There was no introduction other than the handshake; almost at once the very old man spoke.

"In the beginning, when the star sisters came to visit, there was nothing. From time to time, they needed to pass water and left pools, sacred pools from which those who came to understand the Dreaming would drink and learn. Those who learned became the first beings, drawn from the formless and shadowy shapes that crossed the surface of the earth, having only faint traces of what they would become. Then came the sky brothers with their knives and gave shape to these who were to become us.

"Of the sky sisters one only stayed and it was she who created the rise and fall of the land by placing it in charge of the termites who ate into the earth, breaking and cracking it where they would; and so, with the rise and fall of time the great desert was created in which our people would wander.

"These first wanderers carved out the pathways of the Dreaming, which now are visible only to those who understand without thinking, see without looking and hear without listening. My granddaughter is one such. She will go with you and be your guide."

It was all he said. With a smile, drawn painfully from his face, the Elder waved Lina goodbye and she left the shade of the rock for the heat of the desert.

Chapter Ten
PATHWAYS

Bingham was not ashamed at what he'd done, although perhaps, on second thoughts, he felt he should have been; certainly, Lina would not have approved. As far as he was concerned, both men were culpable: if you're not for something, you are – by definition – against it, and neither of the two had done as much as could be expected to find the missing women. Even Bob Evans's posters did not make up for his lack of openness, in Bingham's opinion. If now wasn't the time to call in the police, that moment could not be far away.

He'd had no indication that the constabulary had ever been involved. He wasn't as convinced about the coincidences as he might have led Lina to believe, but it did seem odd, didn't it? If only someone had an idea of where Marjory Fink might have gone – and why – a line of enquiry might just open up.

Evening was creeping on and Bingham wondered how Lina was doing – not that she had anything to do but wait. Wait for what? That was the question. After her 'Desert Awakening' perhaps a 'Sacred Journey' beckoned or she might just make do with a 'Hot Stone Massage'. Bingham couldn't help wondering whether he was wasting both their time hankering after a solution where there'd been no problem in the first place. What was that comment someone had once made? Something to the effect that if there weren't so many people with solutions, there'd be fewer with problems?

It was simply that in the past three years, ever since his search for Natalie Beddoes, Bingham had worried when he heard of an unexplained disappearance; and both cases were unexplained because both women had behaved out of character. Yes, they had, hadn't they? Both women: and for different reasons. Why?

In a sense, all the answers were there in his conversations with those who had known them: Emily Hawker's reassurances, Alice's sighting, Sarah Eastman's feelings, Nellie Doolan's concerns, Bob Evans's brusqueness, Henry Fink's anger ...

Bingham checked that his phone was switched on in case Lina called him. He didn't feel like speaking to her – not yet, not before something, anything, had happened. He'd have to tackle Bob Evans again. He had to be the key. In the meantime, Bingham thought he would wander. It didn't matter where but in the direction of Bob Evans's apartment suggested itself.

This time, he'd walk. It would do him good and save him being ripped off on another taxi ride. He thanked the barman, paid his tab, left a tip for the waitress and set off: not for the outskirts of Alice at first but towards Todd Mall. He wasn't sure why (call it instinct) but once there he knew: it was to buy a bottle of whisky. He'd seen a liquor store somewhere in the vicinity, and he needed to make amends to Bob Evans for his inquisitiveness; besides, Bob Evans might talk more readily after a few tots and he may have misjudged Henry Fink.

The policeman stepped aside for Bingham without question; after all, he was clearly not an Aboriginal and looked exceedingly respectable; but Bingham was as embarrassed as any decent thinking human being would be under the circumstances. He'd heard that the Aboriginals weren't allowed to buy alcohol and that "it was for their own benefit", but to a man of Bingham's generation – the generation that came of age in the 60s – it smacked of riding at the back of the bus. Tony McDonald, whose tree-stacked car had been the start of all these enquiries, had told of being stopped by "a bunch of Abos just outside Coober Pedy" and "the cheeky buggers paying me to get a slab for them. They even tore open the bugger when I got back and gave me a tinnie to be going on with". He'd laughed: it was a way of life and there was no point in fighting against it.

To Bingham, it smacked of humiliation, and thinking about it, as he walked towards Bob Evans's place, he understood the calm shown by the Aboriginals he'd met. He'd always distrusted that kind of calm – aware of the possibility of anger seething beneath – but had been assured it was "in their nature".

The taxi screeched to a halt beside him, throwing up clouds of desert dust from the road, and Henry Fink staggered out. His nose dripped blood and a large bruise was swelling around the left eye and down his cheek; his lips had also lost their sneer and were puffed and trembling as he spoke.

"So much for Bob Evans," he yelled, "I'll teach him to carry on with two women at the same time."

Bingham looked at the young man's hands. There were scraps of skin along the middle phalanges and the knuckles themselves were cut and bleeding. Henry Fink's clothes showed signs of him having fallen to the ground several times: his jacket hung from his shoulders where it had been ripped across the sleeve and his trousers were red with dust.

"What did he have to say?" asked Bingham, ignoring the young man's dishevelled state in a way that struck the other as cold blooded.

"What?"

"Did you find out anything about your mother's disappearance?"

"He denied everything. When I accused him of having another woman, he threw me out. I almost toppled over the balcony. But he didn't get away with it. I gave as good as I got. He doesn't look great himself."

"They were like a couple of animals, mate," called out the taxi driver who had appeared from his cab and was leaning on the roof of his vehicle, listening to Henry.

Bingham looked the cabby up and down, memorising his vehicle number in the process. It would be good to have a witness to such a fight if the police were to be involved, and that time, for Bingham, was moving ever nearer.

"He told me to wait," said the cabby, no doubt guessing what Bingham was wondering, "I wouldn't have missed it for the world."

"Where's Fern?" asked Bingham.

"What's she got to do with it?"

"I wondered where she was."

"You don't take a sheila to a man's fight," snapped Henry, slipping into the stereotype of the Australian man.

Bingham wondered whether the young man had ever used the phrase before that day; he thought not.

"You got nothing else from him?"

"No."

"Was his daughter at home?"

"What's that got to do with it?"

"Was she at home?"

"Not that I saw."

"Off you go, son, and get cleaned up – and thanks."

"For what?"

"For loosening-up Mr Evans."

The cabby laughed and gave Bingham a conspiratorial wink: two older men appreciating a young man's first blooding. He walked round to Henry's side of the cab and held the door for him, not so much out of courtesy, thought Bingham, as a desire to get Henry on the move.

Bingham watched them disappear in the expected cloud of red dust and continued on his way to speak, again, with Bob Evans.

Sunset was approaching, and darkness drawing near in that translucent way it has of doing so in the desert, when the colours merge into one, an almost diaphanous blue so that the stars seem to shine through the very sky.

Bingham was relaxed; night usually had that effect on him when he and Lina walked out for a last stroll of the day, the night surrounding them as though it was a protective shield. He wasn't going to reach an ending with this one, not in the way he had done so before, but he was going to bring it to a kind of resolution with just one more turn of the screw, one more turn of the screw of human kindness. Sometimes that was all it took.

Bob Evans opened the door and his face, not unexpectedly, showed no pleasure.

"I met your adversary on the road, hurrying home in his taxi. He looked nearly as bad as you do – perhaps more so."

"I don't know I'd call him an adversary, but you, I might."

"No doubt."

Bob Evans turned back into his apartment, the towel with which he'd bathed his face in his hand. Like Henry Fink, he'd suffered abrasions: the towel was bloodied and he'd evidently removed his shirt because he stood glaring at Bingham wearing only a vest.

"You told him about Helen?" he said.

"Yes."

"Why?"

"The last time we spoke, the time you threw me out, you more or less denied even knowing Helen Lewis as anything more than a casual acquaintance. It was *Mrs Lewis*, as I remember. Now, I see it's *Helen*."

"What are you implying?"

"We need to get at the truth. You've shielded yourself for too long."

"I wasn't shielding myself."

"That's only one way of looking at it."

"It wouldn't have helped her reputation."

"Was that really the point?"

"I don't see that anything I can say will help find Helen."

"You don't know whether or not that's true, Robert."

Bingham wasn't sure whether the significance of his using the man's full name had sunk in. He waited, nodded towards a chair and sat down. What he knew didn't really matter. It was what this man had to say that counted, and that depended on what he believed Bingham to know.

Bob Evans sighed and slung the towel onto the back of a chair. His smartness had all gone – the polished boots, the neatly combed hair: he could have been any trucker after a long day and a hot drive.

"Who have you spoken to?"

"No one is saying much, but that's often a clue in itself."

"You lied to me, didn't you? You are a private detective, aren't you?"

Where was the anger coming from: anger that he'd been deceived, anger that he'd been caught out?

"No,"

"Then why?"

"For the same reason as you put up your posters – one more turn of the screw."

"I hoped someone might have seen Helen."

"But you feared that they might not have done so?"

"Yes."

"Why?"

"Can I get you a beer?"

"Thanks."

Bob Evans slunk off to the kitchen and returned with two cans of Cascade Premium. He cracked both open and shoved one across the table towards Bingham.

"You don't have a glass, by any chance, do you?"

Bingham was still struggling in the dark, still trying to rile this man further. Returning with the one glass, Bob Evans poured the beer, ostentatiously.

"How much does the kid know?"

"Henry Fink is angrier at his own inaction than at yours. Did you go to the party she threw after her husband was killed?"

"You've been busy."

"I wanted to build up a picture of Marje. Did you know her at that time?"

"Yes."

"And you'd had your own marriage problems?"

"Did Nicky tell you that?"

"People tend to know things in small communities," replied Bingham, not wishing to get the young woman into any kind of trouble.

"I thought I'd buried all that years ago."

"But Marje knew?"

"Yeah."

"And it brought you closer together?"

"Yeah," answered Bob Evans with another sigh, longer than the first and drawn out in desperation. He looked at Bingham and smiled, almost man to man, keen to find a kindred spirit, someone who might understand.

"How many times have you been in love, George?"

"Once."

"Ever been deceived into thinking you were?"

"When I was a young man, a long time ago."

"Do you fancy another beer?"

Bob Evans didn't wait for an answer. He walked into the kitchen and came back with two more cans.

"I'm not the kind of man who plays around with women – whatever you may think, and whatever young Fink may believe. I'm not that man."

"I'd guessed as much … How did Marje find out? Did you find the courage to tell her or did she discover it for herself?"

"I never got round to saying anything. I'm not sure, even now, that Marje knew."

"And Helen?"

"I think she suspected something, but … she put my reluctance down to my first marriage."

"She was keen to take matters forward?"

"She had every right. How did you come to find the letters?"

"It doesn't matter," replied Bingham, eager to deflect the conversation, knowing this wasn't like his other investigations.

"I'd never written letters like those to anyone else – not love letters. It was Helen … she … she brought out those feelings in me."

Bingham came nearer at that moment to knowing one of the missing women by the effect she'd had on this man, a man who considered himself nothing but ordinary: no great lover, just a bloke. He took a long drag on the beer, emptied the glass and cracked open the other tin, noticing the name of the drink – Cascade. Bingham smiled; irony was one of his particular joys.

"Did you come to regret writing them?"

"No – never: they brought out something in me."

"Something you couldn't bring to fruition?"

"It would have been OK given time. There was no rush. No need for anyone to do anything … anything in a hurry."

"But Helen didn't see it in that light?"

"She was different. I was used to … sheilas."

He used the general term as he struggled for a better, something that would describe easier, less complicated women: one you could have a row with, one that would lose her temper and accuse you of running her down in the driveway and then get over it – 'it' being whatever caused the row.

"She never lost her temper, but she was persistent? It was easy to feel you'd let her down?"

"Yeah, that's right. Helen was looking for something else. I was never sure she'd find it in a man – leastways, not in me."

"Was it ever resolved between you?"

"You've read the letters."

"Not all of them, and none fully: I received only glimpses of the truth."

"I was on the edge. I wanted things the way she did, but I didn't want to disappoint her ... you couldn't disappoint Helen."

"She gave you no indication of what was on her mind?"

"I believe she ... I don't know."

"When did you last speak with her? How long was it before she ... disappeared?"

Bingham hung on the word, emphasising his belief that it was not true.

"You don't think she ...?"

"I don't think anything," interrupted Bingham, "But I do know that two women have disappeared and both of them were romantically involved with you in one way or another. I imagine that both of them were putting pressure on you ... in one way or another."

"I saw Helen a few days before she disappeared. I was on my way south to Adelaide. We didn't have long. We never hung around at the Ayers Rock resort, anyway. We just passed the time of day ... more or less. She seemed OK, a bit distant, maybe, but OK."

"Did you meet anyone else while you were there?"

"No one in particular – no one connected with Helen, I mean."

"Where did you speak with her?"

"We didn't drive out anywhere, if that's what you're getting at."

"What did you talk about?"

"I don't know. Nothing in particular."

"Not the idea of marriage?"

"No, there was no chance and ..."

"You didn't want to, anyway?"

"Right!"

"And she gave no indication that she was thinking of going anywhere/"

"No."

"She didn't mention the Dreamtime?"

"I knew she was close to one or two of the Abos. She was impressed with their ... what she called their spirituality, but she never said anything – not on that occasion, not that I remember."

"How did you feel about that?"

"It's out of my league. I've nothing against the Abos but I don't go along with this ancestor stuff."

"Did Helen know your views?"

"I don't have strong views about it. If that's the way Helen wants to go, then I'm OK with that."

"You don't think she may have gone off with them?"

"She'd have said. We would have talked about it. Helen wasn't distressed at me not making up my mind, if that's what you're getting at."

"It never occurred to you to look for her in the desert?"

"You'd be looking for a grain of sand."

"You never drove out the way she might have gone?"

"I'd no idea where to look. Have you ever been out there?"

"You might have asked. Did you inform the police?"

"No one thought it was worthwhile to get the helicopters out."

"Did you ask them to do that?"

"No. I thought the posters might do the job. The people who use the roadhouses know the desert. There was just a chance."

"But a slim one?"

"Yes, as it turned out."

Bingham drained off his second beer and stood to leave. He hadn't come for answers; he'd come to place a man in the context of not one but two disappearances, and he was satisfied or as satisfied as he was likely to be under the circumstances.

He wanted to go home, now – or, at least, back to his hotel. It was a longish walk for an old man and Alice Springs wasn't the kind of place to be wandering about alone at night, or so he'd been told. He looked Bob Evans up and down and thought back to when they'd first met, the day the trucker was dropping off wine for Marjory Fink.

"What are you going to do?"

"I'll write down what I've discovered and what I think and place it in the hands of the local police. There's nothing more I can do."

On his way back, Bingham realised he was still holding the bottle of whisky.

Lina studied the pool of water, listening to Nellie's account of its history. She seemed to know the ancestry of every natural feature in this great Outback: some enlightening, others appalling. Here, the story was of the latter kind; here, a massacre of innocents had taken place when a family group of Aboriginals had fought against the early settlers, whose cattle had churned up the ground, polluting the waterhole and scaring away the wild animals on which her predecessors fed.

They had come a long way since dawn, following the paths that Nellie seemed to know even in the dark of early morning. To Lina, it was as though she was walking into a void; a great, unending blackness stretched before them. It had been cool at first, cool by the standards of the days Lina had experienced and cool enough to keep the flies at bay. For this, she was grateful.

Like most Europeans, Lina had thought of the desert sands as yellow or, in the case of this vast Australian desert, red; but in the morning it was black and lit only by the silvery moon whose cold light cast shadows from the shrubs and ridges.

She breathed in, carefully in case she swallowed something that might be flitting by in the air, and the air was dry and dusty. She couldn't imagine a woman like Helen Lewis being out here alone.

If she listened carefully, Lina could hear the sound of insects. At home, she loved the sound, imagining the crickets and beetles she knew to be moving around the farmyard, but here the sounds, coming from unknown creatures, were hostile.

The sunrise, when it came, revealed ridges that led into escarpments and Lina noticed, in particular, the termite mounds the Aboriginal Elder had spoken about. Following one of these ridges, Nellie descended the side of a hill to where a little stream trickled at their feet. Looking up, Lina saw the smooth sides of the valley down which the now quiet waters had cut a path. The waters that plunged there hissed and splashed against the outcrops of rock, and Lina was reminded of Simpsons Gap. Here, too, in this vast and terrifying expanse of desert, was a special place: a place of rest, a place to quench your thirst.

"A sacred place," said Nellie, "This is one place Mrs Lewis would have sought."

"How far have we come?"

"We have been walking for three hours. It is not far. If Mrs Lewis came from Yulara, she would have come this way on her journey. We can drink and rest in the shade."

Sitting with Nellie in the quiet of this place, the desert seemed less hostile, less frightening to Lina. She began to understand how a woman like Helen Lewis, knowing the desert as she must have come to know it, might have ventured out alone and survived.

"This is one place of the Dreaming, the Waterhole Dreaming, where the three sisters came and brought enlightenment," said Nellie, "I can see her, now, as when she was here – Mrs Lewis standing by the edge of the stream, kneeling, her hands cupped, and drinking."

"Do you hear anything?"

"I only see. There is no sound. There is peace and quiet. The pathway is clear when you are ready."

They climbed the smooth sides of the valley, following a cleft in the face of the rock where the waters had cut a path. Bridging the rise, they saw the countryside spreading away in front of them, the sand stirred slightly by an invisible breeze, and they felt the first flies of the day settle wherever their skin was exposed.

They continued, Lina walking steadily behind Nellie who seemed to glide across the flat desert, a seemingly endless vista of grass, broken by shrubs and the occasional tree. Colours changed as the sun rose further in the sky from the purple of a plum to a dark and, later, a rich red, and the shrubs and trees turned from the dingy green of early morning to a sandy yellow and, finally gold.

Lina thought what a terrifying and desolate beauty the Outback held; and yet there was life. She heard the sound of what Nellie described as the "cheeky bird", the kookaburra, and flocks of finches crossed their path more than once.

Back home, when she and Bingham took on long walks, there were always signs of those who had gone before – trodden grass, gaps through hedges, broken branches – but here there was nothing to suggest that anyone had passed this way. Nellie seemed to walk on in a dream, sensing what might appear, unseen but not unknown.

It was a surprise to Lina when the land dropped before them and, suddenly, they were in a valley, where a second, secret waterhole appeared, served by a spring that bubbled from beneath the earth. The place was cool and served by trees, thick-leaved trees that Lina took to be some kind of eucalyptus, resistant to the ravages of the sun.

Nellie smiled and beckoned Lina to cup her hands and drink.

"We have come far enough," she said, "This place is as far as a white woman would go in the desert."

"You brought Mrs Lewis here?"

"We went further, but she would not have done so alone. We are many hours from Yulara."

Lina wiped the sweat from her eyes. Looking up, she shaded them from the glare of the sun as it peered down from the ridge. They were in the shade of the hollow and Lina was glad of the rest, but there was something strange about the place, something verging on the malignant. There was no reason for such a feeling: they had everything they needed to survive the day.

"It is death," said Nellie, as though reading the other woman's mind.

"I'm sorry," replied Lina, wondering why she used the word. What was she sorry about? Was she sorry or was it simply a reluctance to believe what she heard?

Nellie had walked off, away across the foot of the enclosure towards a group of bushes on the far side. They were thick there, luxuriant compared to those that thrived around the waterhole. 'Understand without knowing': the phrase used by the Elder came back to Lina as she watched the back of the Aboriginal woman disappear among the dark green leaves that shuddered as she brushed through them.

Lina looked up again. The sides of the hollow rose steeply, the layers of rock pressing down, one upon the other. Among the lower rocks ferns sprouted from little crevices and yellow moss glistened on the damp surfaces.

Lina waited. She had no reason to suppose anything was amiss, no reason other than this sense of foreboding that had descended quickly on this sacred place. This feeling rested not so much in the hollow itself as in the movement of the Aboriginal woman as she walked off, and that was how Lina thought of her now – not as Nellie Doolan, who cleaned the apartments at Yulara but as someone from another time, perhaps another world, whose instincts were honed to perfection, who perceived life, and death, through quite different eyes. 'To everything there is a season, and a time to every purpose under the heaven …A time to kill.' Was there ever such a time?

Nellie Doolan's face was stripped of all emotion as she returned from the far side of the hollow, making her way round the edge of the pool and, finally, kneeling before Lina so that the white woman had to look directly into her eyes, eyes that seemed to accept death as a natural step on the path of life.

"Mrs Lewis rests," she said, "but the grave is shallow and the dingoes have been hungry. For you, it is a time to mourn."

Chapter Eleven

TWILIGHT HOUR

Lina and Bingham sat in the Brigadier's Bar of the Reef House Hotel in Palm Cove. They were there for a five night stay before flying on to Sydney. Their visit, in three days' time, to the Great Barrier Reef had been planned as one of the highlights of their Australian holiday, a dream long cherished.

He was playing backgammon with one of the other guests; Lina was chatting at the bar with a group of women the old barman was entertaining with his stories. Neither Bingham nor Lina had their full attention on the job in hand, which was unusual: no one was more focussed than Bingham when playing the game, and no other woman had Lina's ability to hold five strands of conversation in her head at the same time.

The Reef House was just steps from the Pacific Ocean and still cherished the tradition whereby guests were trusted to help themselves to a drink and sign a chit in the tradition of a naval officer's mess. Each evening, candles were lit throughout the hotel to denote Twilight Hour and travellers met in the bar over a glass of complimentary punch. Topping this for Bingham should have been the discovery that Bob Dylan had once stayed here: his name was in the guest book and his photograph on the wall.

This should have been their dreamtime had events not dictated otherwise.

Before leaving Alice Springs, Bingham and Lina had both made statements to the local police, leaving those officers with a murder enquiry on their hands. They had also taken a taxi out to see Sarah and Stan Eastman, not so much in order to bring them up to date with events but more to set up a channel of information. It was Bingham's view that if they were to keep in touch with what had now become an investigation they needed a reliable informant and Sarah Eastman seemed to him to be the kind of woman who could sift news from speculation.

Events had moved rapidly once Lina and Nellie returned to Yulara, events that side-lined Bingham's enquiries and made it pointless to delay their flight to Cairns any longer; and events had moved equally rapidly once the constabulary got their teeth into the search for a murderer.

Sarah Eastman's emails – holding information culled from newspaper and radio reports, conversation at the golf club, gossip in Todd Mall and friends-in-the-know – arrived regularly, the first on March 27th.

Dear Mr and Mrs Bingham,

It looks as though the finger of suspicion is pointing at Bob Evans. According to what people are saying, a bracelet on Helen Lewis's body has been traced to him. It was a gift to her on Valentine's Day. Only a few weeks ago! In one of the pockets of her jacket the police are said to have found a letter also from him and they have found other letters in her apartment. They must have identified the handwriting. The newspapers and the television people are saying that the police are pursuing 'lines of enquiry'. That's all I know at the moment.

Kind regards,
Sarah Eastman

The second email arrived two days later:

Dear Mr and Mrs Bingham,

I hope you are both well and enjoying your stay at the Reef House. Stan and I stayed there once on a second honeymoon and it is a lovely place.

The gossip going round is that Helen Lewis was strangled. What does that suggest to you? Stan said at once that it must have been a thwarted lover and it looks as though Bob Evans is as guilty as sin.

There is no other news at the moment but I thought you would like to know ....

The third email dated March 30th was waiting for them when they returned from their visit to the reef. After some initial well-wishing, it continued:

... Henry Fink has been taken in for questioning. It seems he had a fight with Bob Evans over his mother. We all knew, of course, that Bob Evans and Marje were 'involved', shall we say, but we never guessed that Henry cared enough to fight someone over it. He has always been selfish, right from his schooldays. Anyway, it looks as though Bob Evans and he had a real set-to. This is according to a taxi driver a friend of Stan's knows. It looks as though Bob Evans was carrying on with two women at the same time. I told Stan, if he tried anything like that ... Well, I will leave you to guess!

"What do you think, Bing?" asked Lina, not for the first time, once they were back in their apartment, overlooking the tropical plants that surrounded the swimming pool and enjoying what they both loved most, a quiet drink together when they could talk and just sit.

"It comes down to the motive, doesn't it?" answered Bingham, "Did Bob Evans feel desperate enough to commit murder? It's happened before, of course, with less imperative to kill. Like the police and everyone else, we can only await the forensic evidence and see if that's enough to convict.

"One thing is certain, since they seem to have read the letters Bob Evans wrote to Helen: they police will have questioned the staff at the hotel in Adelaide where they spent at least one enjoyable weekend."

"I'm going to call Nellie. She'll be worried sick."

"Now or after we've eaten?"

"Now!"

"In that case, I'll go and save us a table at that Italian restaurant we saw on our first night here. It's bound to be busy tonight with everyone back from the reef. I heard people say they were going to splash out."

The intense, dry heat of the interior was replaced by a wet heat on the coast. Bingham noticed on the thermometer kept at the hotel that the temperatures had dropped from 43 degrees to 36, but the humidity left him dripping wet after a few minutes out of doors. Noel Coward's line 'though the British are effete, they're quite impervious to heat' did not apply to him or anyone else in their group, he thought as he made his way along the sea front to the Ristorante Vivo.

When Lina joined him, her face was one of concern.

"Nellie says that the police have questioned several of the staff at the resort …"

"Including her?"

"Yes – don't interrupt, Bing, or I'll lose my thread …"

"Sorry."

"Nellie says that some of the staff did recall Bob Evans visiting Helen there on several occasions, but Nellie says that they're making it up because no one knew Helen better than her and she'd never seen him. What do you think?"

"Loyalties change in the face of a murder enquiry, and memories are stirred."

"Nevertheless, if the man is innocent it doesn't seem right, does it?"

"Quite."

The next evening, the last day of March, Sarah Eastman's fourth email arrived.

Dear Mr and Mrs Bingham,

You will never guess. Emily Hawker has gone to the police. That's right, Emily actually left her beloved animals to take time off in support of her friend, Marje! She came over and told us that she had never trusted Bob Evans from the moment she clapped eyes on him. Marje has come back, you see, and she went to Emily for comfort. I am afraid that his free and easy ways have undone him. He has been caught between two women. Not a very comfortable place. Everyone is rather pleased. No one likes a philanderer …

"A man with no escape route but one," said Bingham, when Lina had finished re-reading the email.

"What do you mean, Bing?"

"Two women, in their different ways, both desired him, and he was chained, so to speak, to the Stuart Highway."

Bingham got up from the lounger and walked to their balcony. He watched some of the guests swimming in the pool.

"What are you thinking?" asked Lina, "and don't say you're not thinking anything!"

"None of what Sarah has said constitutes evidence. I know that's blindingly obvious but it's worth remembering, nonetheless. Bob Evans may be guilty and if he is and if he's convicted he won't be the first man to go down on largely circumstantial evidence – not when there's enough of it."

Bingham stood by the balcony for a long time, wondering, while Lina poured them both another glass of wine. Since the Italian restaurant had removed the equivalent of £60 from their spending money for two plates of pasta and two glasses of wine, they'd decided to eat in on their last night and had found an excellent take-away at the Jasmine Rice, a Thai restaurant. A trip to Liquor Express, an outlet recommended by their taxi driver, had also secured them two bottles of local wine at £5 each.

Lina handed him his replenished glass.

"There will be forensic evidence, won't there?"

"Yes – perhaps fingerprints, if the dingoes left any, footprints, marks and stains on the body, that kind of thing. It will also determine the actual cause of death and the time ... The police must have questioned Bob Evans, of course, and will do so until they're happy with his account, but they'll certainly get the details of his relationship with both women out of him."

Sarah Eastman took up Bingham's thought on Bob Evans in her fifth email, which they received when they'd settled into their hotel in Sydney on April 1st.

Dear Mr and Mrs Bingham,

The police have let Bob Evans go. He's a tough nut by all accounts and you cannot help wondering what he has told them. Marje will not have anything said against him, strangely enough. She says that OK he let them both down but she didn't believe for a moment that he would harm a fly, let alone a woman. Mind you, where have we heard that before!

Some people in town are now pointing the finger at the Aboriginals. Gossip has it that a girl at the Ayers Rock resort was involved and that the body was found at one of their sacred places. They do not say much, the Aboriginals. They are a very quiet people and keep themselves to themselves, but who knows? Mind you, I do not believe it myself. I am not a racist ...

"I'll tell you this, Lina," said Bingham, "If I'd have known you were wandering those pathways with Nellie Doolan, I'd have been concerned. Did it never worry you?"

"A little, but I trusted Nellie and David and I had the opportunity to speak with – well, listen to – the Elder. He was a wonderful old man, Bing. The Aboriginals are very spiritual people. There is a mystical connection between body and soul, and they are in touch with their destinies in a way that we might once have been."

"Umm," said Bingham.

"Don't 'umm' me, Bing."

"I'm not. Two thoughts keep going through my head. The first is that when people behave out of character, there's always an explanation, and I can only find the obvious one, which has been staring us in the face almost from the outset. Secondly, on one of our visits to the Stuarts Well roadhouse, you said that something struck you as odd. Do you remember?"

"Yes."

"Well, I should have taken more notice of what you said at the time."

That evening, after their walk along Darling Harbour from the Park Royal Hotel where they were staying – that part of Sydney once known as The Hungry Mile, where watermen searched for jobs along the wharves, and which is now a pedestrian and tourist precinct offering housing and restaurants alongside green, open spaces for family outings – Bingham sent an email to the police in Alice Springs, suggesting simply that they pursue their questioning among the odd and the unusual, if they had not already done so.

Chapter Twelve
BACK HOME

A cold, easterly wind was blowing across East Anglia and Bingham stood looking at his beehives, wondering when the temperature was going to reach the essential 15 degrees, which was when he might dare to open the brood chambers. Primroses were in flower, nestled round the roots of the trees in his orchard, and the blackthorn hedges surrounding the fields of the farm that had once belonged to Lina's parents were in full bloom. It was that time of year the old men in the village of Northfield called 'the blackthorn winter'; spring was coming, but not yet.

As he stood watching the day's foragers about to leave the hive, Bingham heard the bell ring – the bell that had once called his children to whatever meal was waiting. Lina enjoyed ringing that bell, just as once she had objected to his using it to summon their children. Bingham looked at his watch. It was nowhere near coffee time, and he was puzzled.

Lina met him at the stable door, which led into their kitchen.

"They've arrested Marjory Fink," she said, "I've just read Sarah's latest email."

Bingham followed Lina to the large kitchen table, where her laptop was open. Lifting one of their cats off his chair, Bingham sat and read what Sarah had sent.

Dear Mr and Mrs Bingham,

We just cannot believe it! They've arrested Marje! What is going on? All we know is what we have heard on the news. It seems we were right and that Mrs Lewis was strangled. Emily thinks they have made a mistake. She says Marje told her she was a bit depressed and went off to Adelaide to drink it off. She still thinks it was the Aboriginals because of where the body was found and because the papers said that someone called Nellie Doolan was interviewed several times by the police. But they let her go and it's Marje they have arrested.

I do not know what to think. All I will say is that it was unusual for Marje to go off alone – and quietly. If Marje was going on a bender she usually persuaded a friend to go with her and with all trumpets blaring!

Ooh yes, and it turns out that Bob Evans had put up posters at the roadhouses along the Stuart. He had put them up about Mrs Lewis but not about Marje. What do you make of that? It is almost as if he wasn't worried so much about the one as he was the other ..."

"He half-guessed, didn't he?" said Lina, "He was suspicious of her motives for 'disappearing' so suddenly. He never thought for a moment that she'd been abducted. I thought it was odd at the time."

*

At Marjory Fink's trial, counsel for the prosecution suggested that her motive for 'disappearing' was to 'throw people off the scent by suggesting that the two disappearances shared something in common, both being dealers in Aboriginal art', and that she 'intended to turn up later, feigning puzzlement as to why people who knew her so well were concerned'. Police questioning supported this allegation.

It was also suggested that she had previously lured Helen Lewis to the waterhole by feigning an interest in Aboriginal culture; examination of phone records supported this assertion.

Forensic evidence showed that Helen Lewis had been strangled, as gossip at the time believed, but not necessarily by a man's hand; and it was at that point the investigators turned their attention to the women who might have been involved. Once the spotlight was on Marjory Fink, evidence gathered from prints, marks and stains found at the crime scene was used in support of the prosecution's case.

She was gaoled for fifteen years.

As the trial progressed, Sarah Eastman sent newspaper cuttings to Lina and Bingham and emailed them on the day Marjory Fink was sentenced. They were sitting in their kitchen over breakfast when they opened the email.

"Heaven has no rage like love to hatred turned, nor hell a fury like a woman scorned," said Bingham.

"It's a shame it wasn't turned on the man. When I think of poor Helen Lewis, at a crossroads in her life, lying dead in that sacred place, it makes my blood boil. She was a very spiritual person, Bing, denied her destiny. I've never met her but I know her well. If she were to walk through our door now, I could fall in conversation with her as though we'd known each other all our lives."

Australian Autumn 2018

ACKNOWLEDGEMENTS

Although this story is a fiction, its key events and descriptions are based on actual incidents and the experiences of people involved in similar situations and circumstances. Anyone wishing to delve deeper into the real world from which this novel is drawn should read:

Thumbs Up Australia: Hitchhiking the Outback by Tom Parry

Nicholas Brealey Publishing 2006

All the characters in this book are fictitious and any resemblance to persons, living or dead, is purely coincidental.